AND
SUDDENLY,
IT EXPLODES

Mark Mizrahi

To stones, inscribed with history.

YOU AND ME.

Let me begin with a simple truth: I love you. Yes, this you know. It's what you don't know that I wish to tell you. The problem, as with everything, is where to begin. Time has created so much distance between us. There are moments, more often than I wish to say, where I struggle to recall you; your mercurial smile, your gentle heart, your love. I don't even know if the memories I keep are real. Forgive me, I am doing my best.

I know where it ends – here, alone, in JFK airport, waiting for a flight. Loudspeakers call out names; weary travelers mechanically follow instructions, everyone dreaming of someone, or somewhere else. It's the great waiting place. Nothing stays the same, nothing remains.

Knowing that does not diminish the regret. I don't know what will. I thought distance would, but somethings hunt you down like determined bloodhounds. Sometimes the only solution is to walk into the center of the storm and let it thrash you like a Raggity Anne doll just so you can come out whole at the end.

I am being vague, I know. I don't want to be. I want to tell you the whole story. Honestly, it starts with you. But that's too much right now. I'll begin with her, the second act.

THE SECOND ACT.

She didn't say anything when we first met. She stared. I spoke. I spoke about the foot, how it has 26 bones wrapped by 33 major muscles, 19 ligaments, and 200,000 nerve endings. I spoke about foundations. About walking. About the ocean. And about marine life. I didn't speak to impress her. Everything felt natural. The whole time she held her stare and it managed to strip away the party that occurred in the background. The party was not shed all at once but bit by bit — a drunk dissipating to our right, a photo installment on the back walls blurring to nothing, hustling bartenders filling orders dimming to a muted buzz — till all that remained were her warm hazel-green eyes. The openness she presented was stunning. It was her naked, unfiltered self. In her presence I was at once horrified and enraptured. Walking away from her I felt desperate and confused, like a child trapped in a well.

I entertained the notion of turning around, finding her and presenting the following idea: "Let me chain myself to you, dedicate myself to those eyes."

Of course that impulse was unhealthy. Of course I didn't do it. Instead I went home with the woman I had arrived with. Life went on.

LIFE GOES ON ...

Two days after I met her, at home on photoshop, my phone rings.

"Get up, let's go. The drinks are getting poured, the women bored, and we are hungry boys with a taste for the night life." Sean says in a booming voice.

"Oh shit, I don't know... I just sat down to smooth out some photos... deadlines approaching..." I say.

"Not an option really, it's going to be Quinn's for sustenance and beer, Liberty for drinks and girls."

"Really?"

"Yes sir, it will be you, me, my money, your glib tongue, and adventure."

"Sounds more like just you."

"Then that caustic sarcasm of yours."

"No, I'll pass."

"It's cute when you think you have a choice. Now, open your door." He demands.

"Fuck off." I sneer.

"Not likely."

I groan, open the door, as he promised he is there — toothy grin, impeccable tailored clothes — the image of a smooth hedonistic god. BMW M3, not mine, his, parked in my spot.

" Always the impeachable host!" He barges in, lungs first, "Now pour poor me a nice scotch or gin. Nothing cheap."

"So I'm nothing more than your favorite bar-tender now, only without the tips. You don't tip me, you're an asshole." I sneer. "Anyway, it's your lucky day, I got a check recently, and some fine whiskey was on sale."

"Pour away then!" He seats himself at my desk with a flourish

In the kitchen, cupboards open. My glasses nothing more than a mismatched collection of mason jars and tumblers from Goodwill. It fit the general aesthetic of my life. Everything disposable. The amber liquid pouring, I sigh. I had wanted peace tonight. Finish some editing, maybe even read. I was always remiss in reading. But that was dead now. Sean killed the idea. Well, make this a strong one for fortification. Remembering Sean's tastes I add water and ginger ale to his glass.

"Did you work out of the house today?" Sean asks, reaching for liquor, examining it once in his hands.

"No."

"What was the last job?

"That runway shoot in NYC."

"Ah, yes… you lucky shit." Sean smiles to himself. "Did you bag a model?"

"And if I did?"

"Then you're a hero."

"And if I didn't?"

"Then you're a wasteful man."

Drink in hand, facing Sean. "You've always had a way of simplifying life to its crudest forms."

Sean nods, "Simply fulfilling my evolutionary purpose."

"Being a man slut?"

"Don't be accusatory, you are no better."

"Yes, But I don't lie."

"I don't lie, I amend the truth. You're too rigid with it, you have to consider its malleability." He shoots back.

"God you're a fucking lawyer." I say.

He raises his glass, smiling, "And a good one." He laughs, 'Cheers!" The remaining liquid disappears in one swig.

"Cheers," I mumble, liquor hard and warm hitting the esophagus, burning as the body becomes excited from the poison and the head light.

"Met a girl a few nights ago." I state.

"Yes, Julie."

"No. Different girl. Met her at the party while Julie was off with friends."

"You little shit, did you sneak off with her?"

"No."

"At least a number."

"Wait… uhm…"

His question ignites a stumbling and frantic search through pieces of paper on my side table. Next, rifling through the pockets of the clothing from that night, still piled on the floor in a corner. "Here…" I hold up a business card. I had forgotten about her number — how she had slid me her card at the end of the evening without my knowing. It was at my apartment door with Julie beside me, me rifling through my pockets for my apartment keys when Julie 'found' the other woman's token.

"What's that?" She had asked me. I followed her finger to the innocent white card in my right pocket. "Ah…" I paused. Thought. "A potential client… An artist who wants their work photographed." I lied.

She nodded and didn't ask questions. We slid inside and shared tea. She left after tea. I didn't sleep with Julie. Instead I mulled the strange woman and her eyes. That night I dreamt of Jaguar eyes contemplating me from the ether.

"Yes, Seems I did. " I answer Sean, card in hand. For the first time I notice how she had written her name, Zoë, and number, on a blank card. Her handwriting was sharp.

"Better than nothing." He says, holding his empty glass in front of me.

"Another?" I ask taking the glass.

"No." Sean sounds wistful. "To Quinns."

"Walk?" I ask

"Sure, we can slum it."

I live on the North Hill, quieter and cheaper than the center, 10 blocks away. We walk, the Space Needle regarding us from its lofty heights, the autumn breeze keeping us cool.

In sight of Quinn's, a Gastropub, on Pike and 10th, boasting fine food, old fashioned bar cocktails, and a general dedication to high-end bacchanal. You could see usual clientele — a motley collection of art students, thirty-somethings with money and no kids, and foodie-populists.

We have arrived at the burgeoning hour — seats filling fast, people anxiously waiting for a complete party to materialize. Giving up on our designs for a table we slunk into a corner of the bar, sitting beside a tattooed woman. She is beautiful and wears a scowl while drinking an amber liquid.

"Whiskey?" I ask, pulling next to her.

"Rye." She answers.

"Good choice." I say.

"Cheap choice." She says.

"Straight?" I ask.

"Straight." She nods.

The bartender comes by, a man dressed in finery — a brown vest with suede in-lay, white pressed shirt requiring cuff-links, suspenders keeping up khakis, tied together by his handle bar mustache.

"Same as her." I order.

Sean glances at me, "Fuck man, I don't know how you do that shit straight," shaking his head, turning to order, "Old fashioned, please."

"Poison you know is better than the poison you don't." I say.

The woman besides us laughs." Preach on." She raises her glass to us both, downs the remainder of her drink. The bartender replaces it quickly with the smallest of gestures from her hand.

Sean begins to talk to her, "I hope you're ok with our company."

"Yes, we are Neanderthalic at best." I say.

"I'm not much better." She says.

"I'm sure you are. " Sean smirks.

"And if not, don't worry, we can wallow in the depth of degeneracy together." I offer.

"How comforting a thought" The woman says.

All together, drink. Rye is warm, oak-like. No food means it goes right to the head, sure-shot. Bar tender watches us out of the corner of his eye. Boyfriend? Maybe? Past lover, Wish-to-be lover? I don't know. Sean ignores the extra attention, chatters on a mile a minute.

"Of course, we couldn't leave you alone." He said.

"Oh, no. Lil ol' me does need some pro-tec-shin." She mocks in an exaggerated Georgia accent.

"Ha. Funny. I'm betting I need protection from you." He intones.

She presents feigned affront. The same banter flourishes in every corner of the pub-bar. Each person dressed in their Saturday best. A room full of horny peacocks, flaunting and chattering in hopes of finding a strong orgasm, or at the least the promise of one to come. Make it so, give them strong drinks.

"You're aggressive." She says to Sean.

"Direct." He says.

"We can certainly call it that, though that sounds like a euphemism."

She's charming, the way she maneuvers through Sean's rapid-fire tongue. Quick, too. Blessed with an acerbic wit. She looks like a heartache, one that can drag you through mud and walk out runway ready.

"Sure, but most of what we say is a euphemism. Really, we just live, fuck, and die." I interject.

"Drinking as well. Don't you dare forget drinking." She says.

"Never." Sean says.

She looks at him, smiling, "You look like a man who needs to be controlled, beaten a little, even. You'd like that."

"Shit, honey, slow down." Sean mumbles, looks away.

"Honey, when did we become so familiar?" She says, shoulders thrown back a little, smug smile.

"Isn't that what we are trying to do." He snaps.

"It's what you're trying to do." She says.

Yes, she's a quick woman. Damn more beautiful up close too. Colorful tattoos on her sleeve and her shoulders make her walking artwork. The devil doesn't own a red dress, the devil has a tattooed sleeve of tsunamis coming after you. Good luck, Sean.

"And you? When do I get to see your peacock feathers?" She turns to me now.

"After I grow them... puberty is coming on late for me." I say.

"I got time. Just keep the tab open."

"That is a fearful proposition."

"Are you afraid of me?" She asks.

"Buy me a scotch-whiskey and I'll mull it over."

"Fine." A flick of her wrist and the Bartender is in front of us. He has puppy-dog eyes. "Two Aberlours, the 10 year,"

She considers something, "and an old fashion." She turns back to me, "That ok?"

"Excellent, though you may be over-valuing my mulling needs."

"Well, whatever you come up with better shine like a new toy."

The bar-tender is still in front of us, watching; he's a hopeful, collecting and parsing every word she says in hopes of finding reciprocated feelings.

"Hey, while you're here, can we get some fired sardines and some olives?" Sean orders.

The bar-tender nods, eyes me with hatred, and turns away. In moments drinks slide in front of us.

Glasses are raised. " To the pensive stranger, and his aggressive friend." She says.

"Cheers," I mumble, drink. " We sort of fucked up on the names, huh. Well, what's yours? I'm guessing you have one."

"I do." She says, patronizingly, "And you two must as well."

"How about setting up a trade? Two for one, good deal." I say.

"My name is worth at least 4 four names."

"I'll give you 3 and you guess the fake one." I say.

"Try 2 real names and I'll consider giving you mine." She smirks.

"Yeah, I already have your scotch... so, I'm ahead right now."

She laughs, "Yes, you do... Well, I'm Laurie."

"That there is Sean and I'm Jaleel."

"Jaleel?"

"Yes. It's Arabic."

She nods, "You don't look Arabic, at least not completely."

"No, I'm only half. Half-Turkish and half-Columbian."

"Odd." She says.

Food is placed in front of us. Polite smiles, then hunger wins and food is devoured. I think to myself, watching her eat with abandon: Careful, you need wits; Sean already gave up, trying to win over a new girl. She looks like a party-girl — patchwork clothes, glittery voice, and vacuous eyes.

"Your friend found a friend." Laurie says.

"So he did. He's good at that sort of thing."

"Can't imagine it makes for the funnest company."

"No? I don't mind. I like watching human games."

"You a writer?"

"Not for shit, no, a photographer."

She nods, considers the implications of my career, continues, "You'll need company tonight. At minimum to even out the ratio."

I smile at her, warmly, "I don't need it, but I imagine it will be pleasant."

"To pleasantries, then," she raises her glass.

"To pleasantries," hers and mine clink.

Food done, bills paid, introductions to the newest girl made, we venture out. Mr. Bartender watches us pack up with vitriol. A reminder: there is something to little Laurie here to watch out for.

Outside, night has descended. Street full of booze-hounds, punk kids, art students, and aimless twenty somethings. Girls wear as few articles of clothing as possible, men sneer, horns of cabs blare into what is surely one of the last few warm evenings before winter comes.

Sean and his girl, her name is Jen or Jane or Janet, are arguing about where to go. I'm content to ignore them. Laurie is enjoying the night, embracing the chaos around us as if it where her lullaby. Good, let them all be entertained. Laurie slides her arm into mine, grabbing a fist-full of hair as well.

"Gentle." I say.

She laughs and says nothing. To her, my words are worthless. She grasps my bicep. The feeling of her fingers holding me in place are warm, and yet far from comforting. I think now of my dream again: the alluring eyes of a predator cat unsettling me. The teeth, to be avoided at all costs.

"You're not a prolix man." She says.

"Prolix?" I ask.

"You're not a mouthy mother-fucker who likes his own voice."

"I can see that. Sure."

"Anyways, look brighter, you have arm candy, a free evening, and, well, arm candy; it's not a prison." She says.

I smile. She's right. Learn to let go. Breathe. Embrace these things — moments. Make it joyful, piece by piece.

"I'd say you're the lucky one, just look at me." I bluster.

"A regular Fabio." She says.

I laugh, "He got hit in the face by a goose. Flew right into his face while he was on a roller coaster for some kind of promotion."

"Karmic retribution for selling fake shitty butter."

"Jaleel!" My name is called. I don't recognize the voice right away. The same voice, again, "Jaleel! Sean!"

Turn around, scan the crowds for familiar faces. I notice the boxy frame first, then the slight imbalanced walk, with a stiff right leg.

Sean yells back, "Icon!"

Icon reaches me. We embrace. "What are you doing in Seattle from far-away Portland?" I ask.

"A girl, man. I followed a girl I met in Vancouver after a workshop I taught." He explains.

"You followed the pussy." Sean blithely states.

"Sure did." Icon says, smile from ear to ear. " Followed it and found out she had a boyfriend the whole damn time. Lives with him and everything. I don't even know till we get to her apartment and it's like 2 in the morning. She's acting all crazy... he's home when she gets in. Asks if I can sleep on the couch. Oh man! It was horrible... So Awk-fest! It was worse cause we had already had sex. I felt so baaaad."

Sean's girl looks at Icon, "Scandalous," she intones.

"Did you stay?" I ask.

"Of course. It was, like, so late and I had no place to go." Icon says.

"You can stay at mine tonight, and next time, just call me." I offer and chastise at once.

"Oh my god, yes, thank you..." Icon grabs my hands and places them in a prayer position, he touches his forehead to my clasped hands, " Thank you." Releasing me, "but, I need to get my things."

"Sounds so fun. Let's go." Laurie says.

"No. No can do. She told me they would call me once they were home.

"Shame. Nothing to be done but drink and wait." Laurie says.

"Party then it is." Sean decides.

"Yeah, awesome, let's party." Icon says.

Before I have my bearings a whirlwind of trading begins. Laurie brings out a flask. Powders begin a discrete migration from person to person. The bitter taste of MDMA is suppressed by the fire of whiskey. Little spoons of columbian sugar, cocaine, float before faces. Down the hatch, up the nose, in the blood... pick-me-up, lift-me-up never come down. Laurie has a wild mischievous smile as her nose gets tickled one last time. I know that smile, in love with chaos.

"What a fine dandy mess we are... " I say.

And we are. Sean's girl-toy is flirting with her cellphone, attacking it with ferocious intensity. Icon is sucking the whiskey flask like a newborn at the teat. (Rock-a-bye-Icon in the tree-tops). Sean is flirting with Laurie. Laurie is fending off Sean with sly little remarks. Movement, staggering and ineffectual occurs. Somehow, it's another bar. Dim lighting makes us luminous. Perhaps the drugs play a roll as well. Icon knows the waitress. Drinks get poured with a heavy hand that tell of industry solidarity — a shared plight of low rent jobs and low escape options.

Laurie watching me intently, "You're only half engaged with everything." She observes.

"A half divorce is easier," I say with a half smile.

She laughs and lets the issue go. Wit as diversion, build in and build up as protection.

"Jaleel!" Sean shouts my name. He's drunk.

"Yes sir." I say.

"You are a pervert." He raises a glass to me.

"Ha, yes, I am, no doubt. A gentleman pervert, though. Makes all the world of a difference."

The raised glass gets knocked back and the amber liquid, and sugary fructose drink disappears. With a smile Sean delves back into the whirl of conversation... each voice losing all distinction.

"Whoa, you were born here?" From a corner of the table.

"For how long?" A second voice blending in.

"I don't give a shit about him right now." Like harmonies they build atop each other.

"Fuck that." Fuck what?

"I'm too drunk to care." About?

"Text her." No.

"Where was that?" A place.

"We met in the, uh, wait, shit, was a festival."

"Five days."

"She was on a shit load of drugs."

"Hell, I have no idea, something crazy like 4 or 5."

"P's and Q's.. It's a British phrase that means mind your Pints and Quarts... it was meant for bar-tenders..."

Listening I feel distant. The voices seem to be flung toward me from a disembodied periphery, all of it trying desperately to reach me to only fail, and instead pass quietly without incident.

And then it's done. The words replaced by a heady thumping bass. Alcohol is being pushed into my hands… it's Laurie, Laurie is responsible.

"Sour-pus, follow me." She says, pulling.

Nod to indicate complicity; follow the lovely woman.

She pulls us up a small flight of stairs to a loft. Below us: the pulsing Saturday dance zombies, beats not brains Icon would say, limbs flailing, some with grace others just.

The location begins to piece together. It's the Baltic Room. Our arrival method is lost on me. As I try to piece it together Laurie pulls me deeper into the dark corners. "Here, take it." She pushes a small square bag of powder into my hand. "It's Molly, finger her."

Ok. I do. The bitter root beer tasting chemical makes me shudder to the base of my pelvis. Sweat starts. Laurie pulls me closer. I examine her tattoos, become lost in the wave that crawls up her sleeve. I think: Run, it's too much water to take on — the under-tow alone will kill me.

I feel it, gallons of water flowing above me. The pressure is immense. Try to fight it. No fighting it. Fight. Scream. No words, voice overcome by water. Water in your lungs, your ears, your nostrils. Breathe, damn it. Breathe. The breathe returns. The drugs are there, waiting to dose me with a hit of good clean fun.

"Shit, this is good." I mutter.

Laurie laughs, "It feels good. I normally just drink."

"Drugs." I slur.

The rolling waves come internally, first the chemical, then the rhythm of the bass follows. It's a two step beat, heavy drums with an old samba jazz melody and a modern soul. The voice over the track, once a saccharine angel sounds submerged. Everyone is a submerged angel. Love them all.

Universe or God or Cosmic dust, love us, give us meaning.

Outside, cigarette smoke escaping, bright lights, big city; downtown shimmers like a mirage, puget sound black like an obsidian mirror waiting at the edge, reflecting the madness.

Look around. The same faces every week, hopeful. Everyone trying to find the light at the tunnels end. Keep tunneling. No, not everyone. Some people are people, smiles are real. You can't tell from the surface. You don't know what the depths hide. Maybe nothing, maybe something. Smile, I tell myself. Smile. It's so hard. Damn it, I miss you.

"There you are." Laurie grabs me, smiles like a hyena. "Let's go." She's the predator, I'm the prey. Let's give her another notch in the four post bed.

When morning comes I think about you. Then I think about the dream — the same one, the same eyes — judging me, maybe, hunting me, certainly. My phone is flashing. 7 messages wait.

Julie, (12:00 a.m.): The other night was fun, let's do it again.

Sean, (1:45 a.m.): Where are you?

Julie, (2:25 a.m.): You awake?

Sean, (2:30 a.m.):You left, fuck you.

Icon, (3:30 a.m.): Have my stuff. At Sean's.

Sean, (4:00 a.m.): We took your booze hostage. In our bellies.

Client, (9:45 a.m.): Todays afternoon shoot now rescheduled for Sunday.

It's 10:40 a.m. All the particulars are hazy. My head hurts. I'm not home. The sheets here are cleaner, smell of lavender. Tall black leather boots sit beside a full length mirror with white trim. A small library is in one corner, stocked with the poetry of Neruda, a biography of Marilyn Monroe, short stories of Hemingway. On the door is a poster of print I know, something recognizable to most liberal arts college students — a red-headed woman embraced by a moor.

"It's Klimt," Laurie says, "Lovers or some shit... I don't know. It's sexy." She smiles at me. Beautiful as the night before, fangs still intact.

"Woman don't usually take me to their home for ..." I say.

"Coitus, you mean," Laurie shrugs. "It's easier. I can kick you out when I see fit, and I know where all the knives are. Control, I guess. I have more here."

"Makes sense." I spot my clothes piled on the floor beside me. My shoes are not there.

"You're a good fuck, you know?" Laurie states the way someone comments on the satisfactory nature of a cup of coffee.

"Glad to hear the rumors are true." I say. I laugh, which is a reminder of how much my head hurts. "I feel like what the cat dragged in."

She sighs, lays back down, and mumbles, "Drink water… and get me some."

I oblige. Find my way to the kitchen. The cups are organized meticulously by size. I grab two and place one under the running faucet. From her kitchen I can see her living room. The sun is cutting into it, a sparsely furnished space — only an ottoman and a bookshelf — with art prints plastered on every available inch of the walls. Many of the prints are of old Japanese woodcuts, including the iconic waves by …….———— . Getting lost in her wall the feeling of drowning returns. Naked, in her kitchen, I start to panic. The cold overflow of water from the cup shakes me from anxiety. Steadying myself I drink a cup full of water down like a shot. Refilling the cup, then hers, I return to the bedroom. She's asleep. I leave the water on the stand beside her, quietly dress, and slip out into the day.

How many nights pass me in this cat and mouse game? Different faces, bodies, mouths, always new. I don't know anymore why. A habit, really. Temporary remedies, like a bottle of whiskey and Johnny Cash records. Nothing lasting longer than four months before I drift away. I want to say it's a fear of spoiling some pristine garden I am witness to, that I can't tend the garden. Or maybe it's always the wrong women. Choosing is not my strength. You keep me reminding me it's none of those things, at least not precisely. That there is a root to the problem, you seem to say. You, in your silent way, remind me it's the losing. Losing myself, my precarious grip on stability, my freedom to run. I'm in love with lonesome trains, the feeling of tracks moving beneath me with no concern for where; trains bound for empty stations, places where names are no longer legal tender but foolish dressings. There, in that lonely town, maybe you'll finally fade away — disappear with everything into the fog we all came from. Don't fade. Don't leave me. I'm crying.

WHY DO WE CRY?

It's vibrant on the hill, Cal Anderson park is filled with the carpe-diem sun worshippers. The blue open skies so rare that every category of human seems to have managed to stumble out. Punk kids and students are drinking cheap alcohol, nursing hangovers, slack-liners play balancing games between two indifferent trees, various shapes of athletes dash around playing soccer, and the basketball courts are filled with hipster bicyclists playing poor-mans polo.

From the shade of a tree I watch it all. None of it really interests me. Instead, I wish for a book. A camera. Anything to distract me from the rambling thoughts and the head-ache that plagues me. In my pockets I find the card from Marie. She wrote her name in flowing cursive. I text the number she gave me — 'Tea?' I stare at the phone. It says nothing in return.

An hour later the phone beeps. The illuminated screen does not bring the response I hoped for. It's Icon. 'Lunch?'

'Yes.' I reply.

'Give me 30 minutes.'

Sleep overcomes me. It's a restless sleep. The jaguar eyes are there, never wavering in their study of me. I wake with a start, sweating. The stench of day-old chemical and booze seeps from my pores.

10 minutes after waking Icon appears. He's smiling, looks worn thin. "Zoomby!!" He mutters.

"Zoomby." I call back.

"What up dude... where did you go?" He asks, his potato face scrunching in mock concern.

"Home of the temptress... red dress and all." I say, standing to greet him.

"Oh, man. But you're here! Now! That's excellent." He hugs me.

I smile slightly, "Food?"

"Oh, yes, please. So hungry."

"Thoughts on where?"

"Anywhere. I will follow you. You always make a tasty choice."

"Still vegetarian?"

"You know what? No. I eat meat."

"Lovely." I start to lead, destination clear. First feelings of clarity this morning. Strong coffee, crisp fresh baguette, salty sardines at Cafe Presse all I want.

"Man I've never been here. Looks nice." Icon says, absorbing the revamped warehouse with exposed beams whose aesthetic mimics Parisian cafes.

"It's cheap as well. Art ain't free and it pays worse."

"I feel that, so under-appreciated."

We wait at the front, the tables are packed. Two seats are open at the bar, a nod from the hostess invites us to sit. We sit. Icon's fingers begin to dance in the air, bursting in and out of shapes.

"I could never tut, that's so dexterous." I say, admiring him.

He stops, places his hand on my shoulder, "Dude, It's ok. You have your whole thing with the photos." Icon counsels. "Seany showed me some of your prints. They are so good."

I eye him quizzically. "Which ones?"

"Uh... " He placed his finger on his temple, a large silver ring covers his eye, " the one in the alley-way. And uh, the long blue pool."

"Ok." I say, eyes darting across the room. I hated compliments. "I never knew how to feel about those."

"Dude, that there is real art... I mean, like, you're never happy. You're always trying to get better at it, so you can only see the little things that are wrong in it."

Orders are made. Coffee arrives. Silence as we engage in a ritual dressing of the coffee, cream and honey.

"Plans while you're here?" I ask.

"So... I was thinking of filming a dance seen at D's grave. Something... I dunno ... like spiritual. I just want to make sure its not dis-respectful or nothing."

I recall D as Icon speaks. I remembered her. She was a quiet tender soul, very much the mother hen — always trying to care for those around her. We had met before I left the city the first time, back before I knew how easy it was to pack up and slip away, leaving behind the untidy realities too difficult to face. News of her death — the car crash, Icon's surgery — reached me by e-mail while I was in Morocco. Looking at the words laid out on the screen I had no response, instead the cursor hung over the delete button as I contemplated what it all meant, wishing life was as simple relegating brutal truths to an electronic graveyard. Its not. I didn't need you to tell me that. But you did. You do. Everyday I still hear your voice reminding me.

"I think it will be nice." I tell Icon.

"Really?" Icon is bothered, "It's just, I want to ... I dunno, be honest and not disrespectful."

"I know you'll be fine." I say. Icon was too eager, too clean with his intent to spoil it.

"Jaleel! Icon!" A voice breaks the contemplative trance we are in.

"Rachel?" I turn, lazy brown eyes and wild curly hair greets me. "You're working today?"

"I am. But I can stay for a few to say hi."

"Lovely." I say.

She hugs Icon. The two begin a break-neck exchange of auto-biographies. They close the gaps in times with short sentences and little bursts of reconnection. Watching them strengthens a feeling of isolation in me. Rachel leaves us to clock in. We pay, spill out into the wild. Icon begs off and walks away to his next adventure. I don't know when he is going home to Portland.

PARIS, I, TOO, LOVE YOU

A month passes and October's grey biting cold descended on Seattle. The month prior had drowned itself in deadlines. There was a short trip to the Bay Area for a product shoot with Apple, a job infinitely less sexy than it sounded. Also a woman I had been seeing for a few months, most often late night, told me she was engaged. The brevity of her courtship with Mr. Right surprised me, but I wasn't hurt. November and December looked much the same, with a month long trip to London and Paris coming up in January for a few high paying fashion shoots. It looked like a simple time ahead of me.

I try and savor these times. Enjoy the solitude afforded to me for the next 2 and a half months. Distractions are something I avoid. So when my phone rang, and the number was not one I knew, I hesitated before answering.

"Who is this?" I ask.

"Je M'apelle Zoë." A voice I don't know tells me.

"Je suis no hable Francais." I say. Recognizing the name. Recalling an outline of her.

"Good, I don't speak it either." Zoë says, she pauses. "You remember me?"

I do, now, "I'm surprised you remember me." I say.

She clucks into the phone, let's quiet hold space, "There are 28 bones in the foot." She finally says.

"How do you know?"

"Research." She says.

"Research?"

"Research." She repeats.

"Don't trust all your sources."

"No?"

"At the very least get references."

"Oh? … So, who do I call then?"

"No one who would give you a glowing account or a reputable one for that matter." I say.

"What about getting to know the source material myself?"

"That sounds better. At least more thorough."

"Great …" She says. " …So, maybe dinner then?"

"Yeah … let's see … I have most nights free."

"Ok. How 'bout now?"

"Now?" I'm perplexed.

"Now ... yeah, I'm hungry."

"Well... uh ... I haven't eaten. Sure, I can make something."

"Great!" She exclaims. "Text me your address ... it'll be like 45 minutes."

She hangs up. The phone begins a dial tone. I close it, and text her. I stare at the text log for a moment, just two messages from me to her: one asking her to tea, the other my home address. The screen goes black. Staring at it provides no clues as to why she called now. The mystery is better left relegated to the back corners of my mind. More important is answering the immediate anxieties her call has created: what can I make, is it appropriate, does the apartment look presentable, do I?

Then, beyond those surface concerns, is the same dream that had been plaguing me. In the last month the dream had become more vivid, more consuming. Always, only, darkness and the jaguar's almond shaped eyes, menacingly tender, always present — providing me with only the clarity of my inadequacy. How often, in that watchful night, did I call to you, cry for you, cry for me; not once did you respond, not once did the watcher leave me alone with my suffering. I didn't care about the watcher's intent, whether benevolent or malevolent. I only wanted peace.

One phone call is all it takes to snatch peace away, now, and then. So she is coming, Zoë, and the dreams that haunted me found a way to tease me in my waking hours. At the grocers, 2 blocks from my home, some so called serenity overcame me; all that I needed to do was cook, nothing more.

She arrives as the garlic begins to sweat in the butter. I have just enough time to open the door and return to the demanding sizzle before it burns. Kale cools the butter, and wilts the leaves. Out of the oven comes a cast iron bearing a whole roasted trout. Pinches of salt, pepper, oregano, fly from my hand to dress the fish.

"Smells nice." She says.

"I hope it's ok. I don't know if it is ok."

"It's great." She smiles at me. I feel light when I see her smile.

Yes, it's great. Magnificent in fact. For the first time in years I feel nervous. How often had this scenario occurred? It was a basic formula with 1 unknown variable: the woman. You carefully group the known entities — multiply, divide, add, subtract, — then presto, the unknown variable becomes known. But now was not so basic. It reminded me of Arabic, a language flung through the corridors of my childhood, familiar and yet, unavailable to me now. How often I wondered at the secrets of that harsh beautiful cadence. Once I had known it, once I could share it, embrace it. Once. How cruel time is — eventually taking everything.

"Do you always cook like this?" She asks

"When I have someone to cook for, yes."

"Your not just tryin' to butter me up and once I'm all buttered up you'll stop?"

"I like caring for people. At least, I think I do." I say. I try to smile. I feel unsure. It was you who always cared. You who was always ready to give to others, to share from the depths of your knowledge, to create, to engage. I'm simply trying to live up to the standard you set.

"It's good to care," Zoë says, "it gives us a purpose and helps keep us healthy." She speaks with a soft gentleness.

"Maybe it does. I like it. Most of the time." I say.

She nods. "The food is really tasty. I'd eat again with you." She reaches across the table and rests her hands on mine. She smiles, then picks up the plates and walks them to the sink.

The empty chair she left upsets me. I follow her into the kitchen and watch her clean. Zoë moves deliberately, with an engaged grace that seems to think about each action. It is pleasurable to witness. She stacks the dishes, moves over to me, and, with the tips of her fingers, touches my forehead. Everything in me relaxes.

"What now?" I ask.

"I don't know. Anything is ok." She says, her fingers still resting on my head, gently sliding upwards towards my hairline. Her touch resonates through my spine. I shake my head, breaking the connection.

"I can get a movie. You can come with me to the shop, or just wait here… it's around the corner." I offer.

She looks around, "I'll stay, you go."

My coat slips on. Gingerly I open the door. Looking backward, she's begun languishing on the couch, perusing a photo book from my library. The book is of Israel. I smile at the scene, so natural and framable. The wind shuts the door, me on the other-side. It's cool and dark. I am afraid.

Walking I attempt to recall words you used to comfort me. Memory brings me only the peal of your laughter. This is enough to soothe me. The video shop is an old brick firehouse. Inside two thin cashiers greet me then continue talking about some small intrigue. By habit I am in the foreign film section. The selection occurs without process, as if premeditated. Settling with the cashiers, I am in the cool dark again and nearly home. I reach my door in half the usual time.

The key slides into the lock. I hesitate. The jaguar returns to my thoughts. Once, in Panama, years ago, a Jaguar crossed my path. It was midnight along the forest trails; I was with a young biologists who was seeking frogs for an air quality study. She had asked me to join so I could carry her light. I was in the same village documenting clear-cutting practices for Nat-Geo. Somewhere along the trail our light went out. It was pitch black. Nothing could be seen, it felt as if everything — her, my body, the earth — had dissipated into the blackness. As we fumbled with our packs for the back-up lights I noticed the sheen eyes. They were fierce. It was the Jaguar, the spirit walker as the villagers called it. That night it left us alone. For weeks after I prowled the trails at dark hoping for a second glimpse of the creature.

I turn the key, open the door. She is sprawled on the couch. I pause at the entry-way.

"You look frightened," She teases.

"Just pensive." I say.

"About?"

"Shit, I dunno, nothing I have words for…"

"Give it time."

"Ok."

It's quiet. I don't move. She considers me.

"I got Paris, I Love You" I say.

"A French film? Is that a joke?" She asks.

"Well…" I smile, "It's good. It's all short films from good directors about love and loss, and …" I shrug, "Being human."

"Sure." She says. "Let's watch."

The dvd slides into the computer. I bring a blanket to share. We sit side by side. Together we are warm. The first scene unfolds: An older couple conversing, the woman faints, the man provides an endearing bewildered help. Another scene begins: a muslim girl and a christian boy are attracted to one another, and they learn about each other.

In the dark, illuminated by the flickering images (a marriage recovering from infidelity under the looming presence of cancer, an actress challenging her lover with imagination, a woman confronting loneliness in a new language…) I sense her. There is the soft expansion of her diaphragm, the heat emanating from her core, the wisps of her arm hair brushing me as she finds comfort. We move: sitting to laying, alone to entwined. Somehow she is facing me.

"You're missing the movie." I say.

"Oh." She says, not moving. She sighs.

I kiss her, just barely, on the forehead, "You can stay tonight … if you want."

She closes her eyes. "I don't know… maybe… I don't know." She mutters.

"I'll be respectful... I mean I won't do what you don't want." I say.

She opens her eyes. Studies me.

"As long as your comfortable." I continue.

She smiles. Indulgently? We kiss.

"I'll stay." She says.

I kiss her. "Do you need anything? Sweat pants? Water?"

"Sweat pants would be nice," she says, "water too."

The movie an afterthought — I bring her clothing. She examines the cloth between her fingers and asks for the bathroom and for floss. I oblige her. As I wait, I pace.

In the bedroom, now laying side by side like brothers on a motel bed. Thoughts relentless and apprehensive as the lights click off. No sleep. I breathe slowly, discreetly. Calm, I think, calm. My fingers, of their volition, shuffle like crabs across the divide between Zoë and I. Reaching her body, they wait. A slight response and they dive in, dancing across flesh like they are playing a piano sonata. Her body inches closer.

"Ok," She whispers.

"Ok?"

"It's ok. I don't need to wait to make this feel like a good decision." She says.

As gentle as possible I disrobe her. She I.

Naked, now; exposed, nothing to protect us — just bodies as they were born. Blood pumping, rushing heedlessly. Heat rising as everything but her fades. A tongue darts across exposed skin — the taste of salt, the soft brush of thin hairs. There is the smell of raw earth, of beginnings, of endings: as if spring is renewing; the valley blooming as each ephemeral wild flower plunges into the moist earth, penetrating, seeking succor.

Inside her, desire transforms to fear, foreign notions begin to overwhelm me. I want to tell her, "I love you." I want to. I won't. I don't. I can't. That is it: I can't.

Laying together, quietly. Her content, me bewildered. We sleep to dream and in my dreams I am immersed again in the memories — the intoxicating smells of gardenia bushes and the thick scent of roasting dolma, the guttural poetry of Arabic interspersed with the soft touches of French dancing across the living room. I see, on the counter, the standing pitcher filled with rose infused water I never drink from, and you, there, with me — confiding in me, teasing me, punishing me — you again, you always.

Awake, the grey diffused light of morning feebly illuminating the bedroom. The room is simple — a bookshelf, a bed, a few clothes — leaving the furniture everything could be packed in an hour. Only the cameras I own have any significance to me, those lenses from which I see the world. I pick one up, an old metal Nikormat. I turn it on a sleeping Zoë. She shifts. She looks scared. I don't know of what. I take a shot. I replace the camera.

In the kitchen I make coffee for two. Her voice, agitated, calls out for me.

"Are you ok?" I ask, startled.

"Yes," She looks lost. " I just thought … I don't know. I'm ok." She gives me a wan smile.

41

"I made you coffee." I hand her a mug.

She takes it, "Thank you." She cradles the cup in her two hands, "It's warm."

"I need to go to work in an hour. I'll leave you the key in case you want to stay and run around the hill. Once I leave you can move your car to my spot to avoid a ticket. I'll be back 2 or 3 in the afternoon.

"Ok," She says, not once taking a sip of her coffee.

"You don't drink coffee, do you?"

"No." She smiles, truly, then looks through me. "It's warm though, so I like holding it."

"Sure. You're odd." I laugh. She laughs as well. "You'll be ok?" I ask.

"I'll be fine." she says.

Outside, the sun has yet to assert itself, the sky a grey-pearl. Only after I lived in the Mediterranean Climates — months in Spain, in Israel, in Morocco — did I come to understand the unique palette of grey Seattle's sky used. It was plethora of shades meant for a sky trapped in vivid monochrome for months at a time. I walked by a coffee shop. People inside furtively drank down espressos and coffee. I considered a second cup, I always drank more here, not socially, as is the custom in places where the sun demands retribution for activity, but as reflexive protection against the monochrome sky. Today, though, walking is pleasant. The grey feels more like a soft watercolor rather than the hard black-white results of the darkroom. Once I used to adore water-colors, the free flowing nature they represented, the wildness they could capture. My first real set had 58 colors. It was a flabbergasting number to the child I was. Everyday I painted expositions that had no relationships to verifiable reality, little joyous bursts of color. Of course, later, those expressions transformed into the hard-lined exactness blooming in the chemical baths of the darkroom. It was me hoping to understand, hoping to bring clarity to the abstract.

How many years later? And I still don't understand. Like Zoë. Why she called me. Why she made love to me. Why she didn't drink coffee.

ASKING WHY.

Thinking over the night before led to a distracted shoot. The model I was working with — the shoot was for a hair care product — floundered without a constant stream of affirmations. Out of 400 shots maybe 6 were ok. It didn't matter, I'd make it up in photoshop. It was 2:30 when we finished. I called Sean's cell.

"The hermit himself." He answers.

"Straight from the monastery."

"And why are you calling me during my money hours?"

"Uh … fuck … reason?" I paused to think. "Drinks?"

"Normal humans work at this hour, you know… make money."

"Yeah, I don't think I really want a drink."

"So go home and masturbate, or watch news, or some other moody art shit you like." He derides.

"Some girl is there, I think."

"Seriously? Fuck off, go home."

"Drink first."

"Your priorities are all fucked up... you need a psychiatrist or something..." He pauses. "Yea, I'll get a drink."

We meet at Barrio, at my insistence. It's on the hill, close to home, serves Mexican food in a refurbished warehouse space with exposed beams, and dim lighting, giving it the appearance of being a rustic metal skeleton.
I order first, "Mezcal flight."

Sean laughs, "you got it bad homie. Pussy killing the brain." His laughter is light and piercing. He stops to order, smiling still, "Beer, let's see... Modelo Negro." He smiles at the waitress, "How are you?" He looks like a predator, unflinchingly staring at her. She answers and walks away smiling.

The flight lands in front of me. I smell each one — clean wooden scents, all of them. The first sip is intense, a thicker deeper tasting tequila — cactus sugars gone harsh and electric.

"I used to drink every day around this time, " I mused, "in Israel with a group of ex-soldiers. It was this anise liquor with a side of coffee. This one guy, Tav or Tal, would always have a gun on his ribs held up by a holster..."

"So?"

"Nothing...I just thought about it."

Sean smiles. A smug smile.

"This amuse you?"

"Yeah... I mean, I hardly hear from you this past month, then bam in the middle of the afternoon you call, middle of the day, to get drinks. You get me here then just babble memories from your time of taking photos in a war-zone. It's odd, thats all."

"You don't need to be a dick about it."

"I'm not... I like it. I mean this is better than a desk."

I nod, "I'm a terrible task-master anyway."

"So what the fuck then? Why call me now and reminisce about living in hellish war zones?"

"Shit... I don't know. I miss it? There was a certain clarity there... everything so close and up-front."

"So why the fuck you here?"

"This?" I lamely wave my hand in the air.

"Mexican food?" He says, "They must have that shit everywhere, right? I mean don't they smuggle themselves everywhere? Besides, you need to go to San Diego or LA for real good shit."

"You have a knack for assholery." I say. I shoot down the first Mezcal. It has a bright floral taste.

"I am. I'm an asshole. I even get paid for it. But, that's not the point. The point is: what are you doing here? Just trying 'this'," he mocks my hand gesture, "is not living. That's purgatory."

Sour-faced, angry, the second shot of the flight gets drunk. This one is more pepper-like. "Fuck off."

"Look, I like this shit. I like my money, my car, the women I date. I even like you. But you? You're here, but... not here." He mocks my hand gesture once more.

I don't have a response. A second beer for Sean arrives, also chips and guacamole. It's on the house he is informed.

"Anyway," He continues, light-hearted, "that shit doesn't matter... who the hell is at your apartment? I need to know."

"Zoë." I say.

He drinks his beer, "Who?" He asks.

"Wish I knew. She's just someone I met..." The third mezcal is gone, this one smoky, like a whiskey tequila.

Sean laughs, "Fuckin' Jaleel ... Get your mind straight." He asks for the check, covers it all, gives the waitress his card, smiles and takes his leave.

At the apartment, Zoë is gone. I find a note:

Thank you. You're a pleasure. Again, soon; please and thank you. Yours, M.D.

SO THIS IS LOVE?

I waited for the moment when
the world would bloom
Unfolding across wide expanses.
Then I met you.

The weather turns frigid with fall and winter. Life with
Zoë accelerates. Fear, my own, dissipates. Work, once a
haven, becomes a secondary nuisance. She intoxicates me.
Friends compliment my new demeanor. Clients, whose jobs
are now less painstakingly worked over, are more pleased. At
night I even learn to live with the jaguar — almost trust it. A
new levity infiltrates my perspective. In short, I find myself
lost in love.

There is nothing catastrophic or vastly transformative to
it. It is simple — a smile flung across a room, an elegant kiss
placed on my forehead, the manner in which she cracks an
egg (long fingers tugging at the calcium membrane to unlock
nutrients).

I can recall with tenderness her feral laughter given to me
one evening. I had been reading the works of Carl Jung out
loud. She listened in bed beside me.

"He diddled his patients," I told her.

"Diddled? What's diddled?"

"Sex, coitus, fucking..."

"It's a funny word. Diddled, diddled, diddled..." She repeated the word, turning it into a melody. "Diddle diddle doo, who diddled you?" She explodes into laughter. Her laughter was like ringing church bells calling you, not to worship, but to freedom.

There was also a seriousness, a growing attachment that led to small shared secrets. Where I could, I attempted to be useful. Meals cooked everyday — where had I learnt the skill, she asks? On the road, in temporary dwellings on the way into and out of war zones for work.

She asked about those years, what I saw, what I felt. All I could offer were a few mumbles about nature and an empty stare. She nearly cried then. She has such a tender heart.

Her story, told in pieces. Her family French and German, her fathers adored her. Fathers, yes, two, Jean and Tobias. She was sprung from a surrogate. The fathers split. One, Tobias left for the church, married a woman, moved back to Germany. She remained with her non-Christian father. He raised her in Brooklyn, she took on life. She was a fearless thinker, a loyal supporter of what she believed. Nothing daunted her except her desire for perfection.

Nights, days, bled together as I studied her face — her large reflective eyes, her expressive mouth, her small sharp ears... From her face to her body, my attention never wavering. Sex with her awoke a primal hunger that would overwhelm me. Scents and tastes became heightened. Every cell I housed swayed and bounced in excitement at the thought of her body, at the thought of Zoë.

The full experience of her was like being shot from a cannon. I felt alive. I am alive. And, in love.

Ikea's warehouse, Swedish purveyors of furniture, was where I learned to recognize: this was love.

Zoë asks me over the phone to accompany her.

"You need what again?" I ask, sure she has told me before.

"A bed. I want something adult, not a college kids futon."

"Sounds like you're heading to the wrong place then." I intone.

"Well, it's also what I can afford." She snaps.

"OK … I get it. The bed is nice, it's one of the only things I splurge on usually." I say.

"Great," she pauses, "you can help me choose one."

"Choose one?" I'm taken aback.

"Yes, you'll be sleeping in it." She states nonchalant.

I had no answer. Such a simple statement. Yes, I would be sleeping in it. But.

That was it: but. That word contained the entirety of my anxiety. It contained you. It contained the house we shared; long talks into the night as you would sit beside me, warm drink in hand; the weeks spent at the lake home; the lost necklace we hunted, tearing apart every crevice of home. Home. I hated the idea now. I hated what home meant. You taught me we were never safe. Safe is an illusion. Home is an illusion. Zoë was asking for home. A small parcel of one, yes, but home. Home needed something I lacked, something more tangible than I felt.

But, I go anyway. She picks me up. We drive. The car is parked. Doors swing open. The bright blue warehouse sprawls before us: Haggard people shuffle out the exit.

"This place is a nightmare." I say.

"But it'll be fun. Besides, you get to lie in bed with me."

"That's a quick route to being expelled." I smirk.

She laughs, pulling me into the blue-painted monolith. We tramp through decorative living rooms, barely pause to examine space-saving ideas for closets, by-pass endless cubicles filled with simple cheap design. We march on slowly, the journey punctuated by little plays we act out in 10 x 10 squares: honey, your daughter has marijuana. I found it in her desk. What now? (Seriousness dissolves, snorts of joy.) OMG, college is like awesome roomie, we should totally go to a kegger... (Laughter.) A puppy? What kind? The best kind. But ... where will we find the space. (Look around at our tiny cubicle ... Laughter, loud laughter.)

Our jocular antics attract silent stares from sad looking adult shoppers and wistful children. The admonishment and longing incites more jovial laughter, till it begins to hurt our bellies. We stumble onward, barely noticing the sleek lamps, cheap desks, couches, and kitchen cabinets that pepper this furniture labyrinth. We gain control of ourselves in the food court, the oasis for beleaguered families.

Zoë exudes excitement, "Let's get Swedish meatballs."

"Fuck no," I spit.

"Jean always took me here as a kid." She's nostalgic.

"Sure, but I'm not your father." I say.

I say something wrong. Silence, thick, like drowning. With anger she turns and stamps off. I follow in her wake, wishing for clarity, any indication of what I did, and when her punishment would end. Before reprieve is granted we stumble into the mattress section. She leads, silently, to a chart that describes the choices. She picks, silently, three. We circle each one, touch each one, lay on each one. Her first words to me are, 'lay down,' when at the first selection I am apprehensive to follow. We lay quietly. She speaks to me again at the last mattress, asking me, 'how much is this one?' Testing and choosing a mattress takes only 7 words, and twenty minutes.

In the warehouse, putting the mattress on a trolly, she stops and stares at me. In a harsh short clip she tells me: "I know you're not my father."

I have nothing to return to her. She forgives me with a kiss before I can conjure words. With tentative smiles we finish loading the mattress onto the trolly. She pays, I bring the car to the loading dock. Loaded, we drive off.

Her car pulls into the driveway of her home, an august woodsy house in Lake Forest Park. The rental house is surrounded by pines and firs, secluded, yet within eye sight of Seattle.

Hours later, after the bed is settled in, after we basked in the shine of after coitus dopamine, we enter the backyard hot-tub. The thin pines protect our naked bodies from neighbors eyes. Seattle's city lights shimmer in the distance. Rain caresses the moist earth.

"I'm sorry." She says.

"For what?"

"For how I reacted at Ikea." She says.

"It's ok, I imagine there's a reason." I say.

"Do you want to know?"

"I'll leave it to you to decide if it's something I need to know."

She watches me, considering my words. "I think you should know." She whispers, each word measured.

"I'll listen." I say.

She bites her lower lip, showing the tips of her canines. "My dad died, three years ago."

"Which one?"

"The only one," She growls.

"How?" I ask.

"Lymph cancer." She says, "He had it since I was 15."

She begins to cry. The soft tapping of rain is all I am aware of now. I pull her close. She shivers, she is frightened. I am frightened. Words build in me, and inevitably feel lame. My lips graze her. A smile feebly begins at the edges of her mouth, only to fail.

Holding her, I feel her clavicle on my chest; the rise and fall of it following her breathe. My fingers sit on the sharp edge of her shoulders blades. The world smells fresh, inviting. All I think about are seedlings.

I don't say anything to her, continue to hold her. Words quaver outward, continuing to tell her story. "It was terminal from the first diagnosis." She stops, gathers herself, whispers, as if to herself, "7 years of my life... we knew he had it for 7 years."

"I couldn't talk to Tobias. He's ... I mean, shit, he just babbled about Jesus. Hardly called ever. Once he even told me it was Jean's punishment for not accepting the Savior and living in sin still. It made me.... Fuck.... I was mad ... and also ..." She stops.

"Sad?" I offer.

"Yeah... but confused. I was afraid and thought that I had to grow up... I mean I was 15." She burrowed herself further into me.

"I moved out eight months after I learned the news." She says

"At 15?"

She nods. " It helped me, kept me busy. Jean seemed to be ok with it. He just wanted me to be happy."

"Where did you live?" I asked.

"With an older friend who went to Columbia. I dated one of his friends. We lived in Washington Heights in this tiny one bedroom. I got a job. Jean helped me with the resume and I did this City Study High School where I got credits for working and writing reports on topics I liked. The whole school thing was hard enough ... but Jean's sickness made it impossible."

"That's intense." I say.

"I guess, but I also thought that being grown up could protect me."

"Did it?" I ask.

Zoë doesn't answer. She cries harder. I continue to hold her. Seedlings need nourishment, the proper balance of nutrients provided by soil, water, and sun. Eventually they grow. But nothing is perfect, every seed suffers. There never is enough of a balance.

WHAT WILL SAVE US?

It's wet, the cold hard rain tapping the ground impatiently. It's been wet for a week without stop now. The coffee shop keeps us dry. The latte keeps us warm.

"...I think the new coloring is going to look good. Brings together her eyes and solve the washout problem from the first template." Geoff says.

"Think Roberts will like it?"

"You know dawg, that dude is tough to read. Like trying to figure out the thoughts of a 2 year old."

I laugh. "How's... shit, what's her name? Tall, brunette, likes to wear boots..."

"Candace?"

"Yep, Candace." I clap.

"Oh man, I dunno." Geoff shakes his head, "I think I like projects."

"Yeah, How so?"

"Just women who come with crazy..." Geoff tsks, "Maybe I'm too nice."

"Maybe they're all crazy?" I suggest.

"Think so?"

"Nope. But it's a nice myth."

Geoff laughs, "Explains the last three relationships."

"You could be driving them to the edge."

"Put that in my dating profile."

"That'll keep them knocking." I say, "You know, I think it's a balancing act: keeping your own sanity, but thinking of others." I pause, "Of course, I have no idea of execution."

"Shit dawg, I know," Geoff's pelican face breaks out into a wide grin, "Whatever though, we shine."

"When it rains," I repeat, teasingly, the tag-line that he calligraphies on every free scrap of paper in a 10 meter diameter of his pen till every inch of a desk reads: when it rains, we shine.

A plate of olives arrives. I begin to pick at them.

"You love that shit," Geoff notes.

"Learned it in the Middle East." I say.

"What was that like?"

"It's ... something I guess. The whole place is sort of wild, teeming, just a little crazy. People really living right there, at the edge of reason and madness." I eat more olives.

"Shit, that's intense."

"I miss it, sometimes, being so close to that feeling."

"Ever think of going back?"

"Don't miss it that much." I say.

Geoff chuckles. He stands, wire frame, six foot tall, gangly long, and excuses himself to the restroom. Geoff absent I review the specs and our work. The center of our piece was a female model staring at you with heroin eyes. Our job was to make her "sex-ready." The actual directive was to turn her into an urban jungle queen. I sigh, push it away. It's all shit. Pure shit.

I think of my old assignments. The shot of adrenaline, the crash of your nerves after. Then, the moment of truth where you look on the film to see what you get. There is no brushing it up afterwards, no careful constructions or tricks that can be used to direct and distract the eye. It's: snap a shot, send it off; back home folks look at it. If the cliche holds true you write a novel in images. Never enough, it's never enough. Words and photos always fail. Anyway, I left that. Now I have "urban jungle queens."

Geoff returns, sits. He asks me about some background color, then a font. After 2 hours we have something workable. It's now night. Pushing work aside, Geoff asks, "When are you going to Paris?"

"3 weeks from now." I say.

"Oh shit, soon brother."

"Yeah, this is my last project before then." I say.

"Time to kick it, Party." Geoff says.

"Nah, not likely... take it slow." I say.

"Still seeing ... uhm, Zoë?"

"Yeah. Still. She likes me." I say.

"Yo, brother, the real question is: do you like her?" Geoff asks.

"I do. It's odd. I mean, there are moments where I feel like she's this hunter carefully tracking me, waiting to capture me.... but, I like it, like her. I do." I say.

"Sounds like a good thing." Geoff says, "Something nice."

"Yeah," I nod, absent-minded, "Let's get a beer, or whiskey... anything but this shit."

"Yeah, brother, I'll invite Sean?" Geoff asks.

"Sure, Icon's still in town too."

Geoff begins a flurry of texting. After some thought, I send one to Zoë. Within minutes a time and a bar are selected.

Geoff and I arrive first. Vermillion, a queer-friendly art bar that pours a healthy whiskey for cheap. Entering the front is a long hallway with hanging art and one table, leading to the back and a dim lit bar. Geoff sits, I continue to the back for drinks.

Returning, Icon is there. He's jolly.

"Oh shit, I didn't know you'd be here, otherwise I'd have you a drink." I say.

"Aw... that's ok. I'll get it." Icon smiles.

Geoff stands, "No sit down brother, I got you."

"You sure?" Icon scrunches his face, "No... you sure ... no, I got it."

Geoff ignores him, is already off to the back in long strides. Icon watches him with a smile. He sits.

"Yo ... how is it?" He follows his question with a complex clapping routine.

"Good, you?"

"Dancing. More dancing. Getting hit up... " Icon opens his phone, shows me a message, "gigs, competitions... I may move up here."

"Yeah?" I read the message, words of praise and gratitude.

"I think so... in like 2 months."

"Shame, coulda stuffed you in my place. I'm off to Europe ... maybe I'll travel."

"For reals?"

"Maybe. Zoë is here. Not sure, I'm thinking about it."

He reaches his hand over, resting it on my shoulder, "You know, you gotta do what you want, man. If that's what you want, do it."

I laugh. "I'll try."

I think about what I want. How difficult it is: to know, to get.

Geoff is back. Three drinks in hand.

Icon's face lights up, he makes a polite grab for one, "O, fuck man, thank you!"

As we drink, chat, Sean struts in. He looks smug and superior -- like always. Clothing is tailor perfect.

I smile, "You look rich." I say.

He sneers, smiles, "You look like you don't give a shit."

"It's nice jeans... and a nice shirt." I defend, half-heartedly.

"Still jeans." he says.

I nod.

Sean sits, greets the others. He disappears to the bar for a drink. At rounds end we pack up and move next door, to Grims, a trendy wood themed bar. I text Zoë the change. We fill a booth, one seat remains open. Some food is ordered. I feel drunk, magnanimously drunk. That wild open feeling is short lived. Just as I begin to enjoy it the confusion begins to eat it.

I am a foreigner here.

I see Geoff, beautiful Geoff so positive so light. I see Icon, always buoyant, always grateful. I see Sean, perpetually debauched, mischief incarnate. I see me, desolate.

Old anxieties crowding in. I wonder: which it will be? Fuck it. It's you.

Always you, always will be. You I am returning to.

I'll never be free, will I?

Will I?

Tell me I will.

Just as the worst begins – memories of conversations, gentle touches, a shared smile, the whole world we built – Zoë glides into view.

I blink.

She is luminous.

She smiles at me, crooks her head to the side, "You ok?" She asks.

I am. Yes, I am. "I am." I say.

"Good." She says, her words sound like a tender laugh.

Laughter surrounds me. I feel light. Turning to the three men I introduce Zoë.

She is welcomed. Icon bows his head, Geoff makes more room, Sean raises his glass.

"So nice to meet you!" Icon proclaims.

She raises an eyebrow, clucks, "Yep. It's nice to meet all of you."

Sitting, the waiter approaches, she considers for a long minute, turning to me, "Do I want to drink?" She asks me.

I shrug, "I like it. I can't decide for you." I smile at her.

She nods, looks over the menu, holds the waiter hostage with a series of questions, picks a gin-based cocktail. It arrives soon, with a new round for all the boys and me.

She sits quietly with her drink, watching us. Even as I talk, jocular remarks flung across the table either to attack or in defense, I watch her. Icon says something and she laughs, light and feathery.

Geoff is nodding at me, drinking, ordering more. A suggestion is made to move on to hear music. All participants agree.

Dancing at Q, the cities new club: a sleek, spacious temple to bacchanal delights. Blue-black lighting frames us as old disco melodies and driving rhythms mix with big thumping bass. Everyone is smooth, dancing. In the back corner, on the left side of the speaker, a small semi circle has formed populated with dancer kids. Icon is among them. Street styles mesh together as old and young share communal space. Each taking turns in the center. In the center is a woman now, lightly tapping to the beat, heel to toe, to toe, half turns mixing with drops to the floor and springs forward. Next: a thin Asian man, in center, carving the air with his arms, dexterously pivoting, and hopping in perfect step to the beat. Like a turnstile, someone new: waves coursing through their body in unison with each step. It's mesmerizing.

Zoë moves within the music, around the music, to the music, against the music. I smile, feel awkward. She approaches me. In a subtle manner Zoë prods me to move, first from my feet, then gradually upwards (the knees, the pelvis, the abdominals, the ribs, the shoulders, the arms, the head) through my body. I begin to dance. It's freeing, new. Feels nice, though awkward.

Songs play on, one after the other in perfect mix; I keep dancing. Icon and I step outside, he's soaked in sweat, smiling, "It's so nice to see you dance," he tells me.

"It feels ok," I say.

"Of course it does, keep dancing." He smiles, hand gently on my bicep.

I laugh, "Alright." I think what it means to him, dancing now after almost never walking. Dancing saved him, he told me once. Good. We all need saving. Something will save me.

"How are you doing?" He asks me.

"You know…" I stop, think, "Actually, I feel really happy, I mean really just happy." I hear myself tell Icon this, and understand it is true, it's never true, it is true; I want to cry.

Geoff and Shawn and Zoë join us outside. It's a cool night. Zoë makes us to walk a half block away from the entrance to avoid the smokers. Shawn gives me his flask, I sip it. Whiskey. The whole thing makes me smile. I'm happy, damn it. I'm happy it, and I love it. Love everything here, all of it, everything as if I was washed out in serotonin. So sweet, so tender, so harsh and intense and perfect. I'm happy, so really happy.

CRUISING ALTITUDE IS 30,000 FEET.

Three weeks later and everything is in order for my upcoming work trip. The logistics are covered: my plane tickets are all in order, I have a small room sublet in London near Portobello, a hotel in Paris, and my own apartment is being sublet to a computer geek on a short term contract with Microsoft. Simple.

My things, the few items I cherish, however, feel less tidy. They are stored at Zoë's. It was an agreement I came into easily, but am now confused about.

My last night, the fourth night at her home, I am intertwined with her in bed, she asks, "Will you miss me?"

"I don't know." I pause, " I mean, I will... but ... I'm used to this. Leaving, and not seeing people... and I don't normally think about coming back, or what that means ... and I guess it's new... and I want to ... but I guess you get used to things one way." I trail off and look at her.

She betrays no disappointment at my answer, concern for me ... maybe.

"I'll miss you." She says it, matter of fact. I'm silent.

Her thin arms across my chest, her body close to mine, her breath slowing, falling asleep, I ask, "Are you sure it's ok? My stuff, I mean?" I ask.

"Hmm? Why not?"

"I ... things just always have a way of ... " I pause, I want to say fall apart, "unfolding when two people are so far. You're not vindictive are you?"

"I don't think so." She says, her body shifts, she's resting on an elbow. I can feel her gaze, "You can call me. We can Skype."

"I suppose." I say.. My answer baffles me. I want to agree, to bond her to me, to create those arbitrary boundaries we are to live by. I say, "I'll try."

She runs her fingers through my hair, hums a soft old world melody. Sleep arrives gently.

Leaving on a Jet Plane ... Don't know when I'll be back again.

The morning is grey, subdued. Breakfast simple yogurt and walnuts with a dab of honey. Zoë watches me intently as I eat, studying me.

"What are you doing?" I ask.

"Trying to memorize your face." She says.

She leans over the table and kisses me.
I look at the clock, "Time to go," I say.

She says, "Ok."

Last check, everything in order? Ok, in the car.

At the airport curb, bustling travelers rushing to wait. She sets my camera bag on the curb, at my feet, "I like you. I even love you. I want to see you when you get back, and I want to talk to you while you're gone. I know you're not sure what we are, but I don't intend to seek someone else." She sighs, gentleness exudes from her voice.

"Thank you, " I say, "I think I understand – and I feel... I mean, I guess... you make me happy, a real happy, and that's new and I like you." I finish, feeling lame. I look at her, imploringly.

What would you say to me now? You always lived without fear. Ok, so, "I mean to say I love you." I say.

She smiles. So fucking simple, so fucking gorgeous – walking away is hard, but I have to.

Luggage checked ... security cleared ... seating done, I settle in. It's a long flight – first leg to JFK, 3 hour lay-over, then Heathrow.

I open my bag, thinking to watch a movie. A book is waiting for me: "The Little Prince." Antoine St Exupéry book to his estranged wife.

The royal blue cover opens, words written by Zoë on the inside:

> Why do we treat the fleeting day
> with so much needless fear and sorrow?
> It's in its nature not to stay,
> today is always gone tomorrow.

Wislawa Szymborska

You deserve to happy.

The note was written on a home made in-lay, thick water-color paper splashed with a vibrant orange center, royal purple edges. To touch it feels textured. Opposing the in-lay is a dedication to Leon Worth.

"I love that book," My neighbor begins, "I gave it to my boyfriend – my ex, I guess..." She trails of, turns to stare at the luggage being roughly tossed into the plane's belly, "Anyway, it's good." She finishes.

I nod, close the book gently, put it away. From my bag I pull headphones and isolate myself. Music, ethereal rhythmic beats, soothes me.

Hours later: JFK. Nothing to do but watch travelers hustle from point to point; they run as if it had purpose, as if their lives meant something. Sure, they do, I suppose. At least it makes us feel better, purpose. No use in mulling. Take what's given, make what's not, keep going till you can't.

Soon: aloft again, 3,000 miles to go. Inside the cocoon of first class now, I take a Xanax and chase it with a whiskey shot. Sleep overwhelms me.

I'm dreaming –

Alone, stretching darkness surrounding me, your name is flung through the air. I give chase, but, the sound echoes. I try and follow, running only into darkness. Legs refusing to stop, heart rate frantic.

The darkness flickers and brightens, illuminating a skeletal city. Nothing is here; and yet, I feel pursued. I run, still. Each fall of my foot shifts the road beneath me as the city is swallowed by a jungle.

Running in perfect step with me, effortlessly, is the pursuer. Faster, faster, I run,… and yet never fast enough.

I wake, covered in sweat, breath short, coming in spurts. My neighbor, a pale-yellowing WASP woman on too many blood thinners, is startled. I order a whiskey and swallow the hard gold liquid in one gulp. The captain comes on the loadspeaker. We will be landing in thirty minutes, the weather in London is weather, enjoy your stay. So, our descent has begun. Yes, yes it has captain. Let's descend.

COUNT ALL YOUR FRIENDS, ME AMONG THEM.

The next evening, waiting in a small dingy pub next to the sub-let I'm renting. The lighting is snug & evil. Stale beer dominates the senses. Across the table is John, a thin-ginger I've known for years.

"You look mischievous as ever," I say.

"Ah, ha, I learned from the master." He smiles.

"Introduces us sometime." I say.

"I'll just get him a beer." He says, and, with a flick of his wrist he manages to have a beer dropped in front of me.

I look at it, pick it up, "Ok, as long as it doesn't approach our last night in Cairo." I pause, "I work tomorrow."

"Yeah?" He smiles, "So do I." His glass raises into the air, ours clink, then a quaff.

"Where now?"

"University of London, School of Economics." He says.

"Studying?" I ask.

"Micro-Economics of Third-World countries and development programs." He says.

"So, a mouthful. You like it?" I ask.

"It's a good program." He says.

"Ever the tender diplomat." I say.

"How's that?" He asks.

"You managed to run Humane Programs in war-zones, negotiating with everyone and still remaining emphatic... that's a sort of tender diplomacy." I say.

He laughs, "Yeah, but these kids here, Uni? That's brutal."

"Well, you are here, that is impressive ... Good Ol' Virginia boy in the big city." I say.

"Ah, yeah, USAID is very generous to me." He says, "But you ..." he chuckles, " Look at you, fancy new gig in fashion, flying round the world."

"I was before." I say, dismissive.

"Ah, only before you didn't know if dinner would be six feet of dirt." John says.

"Uh huh, the general level of safety has increased, not to mention that the accommodations are nicer, I suppose." I smirk.

"Well, sure, you get to keep all your limbs." John jokes.

"Lacks that quality of adrenaline, though." I laugh.

"Nothing like a shot of adrenaline to help you sleep." John says.

"Steady diet of it... it's how I kept all my luscious locks of hair." I say.

We order a second set of beers. The waitress asks where we are from. John answers, smiles. She laughs, turns to fill our orders and work.

"You need to write a thesis?"

"Yeah ... sort of ... a report on the shifting relationships or power dynamics between resource rich third world countries and the first world and how that affects the purchasing power of villagers... or something like that."

"OK. Give me the short of it."

"The short of it?"

The beers fall between us. We each take a quaff.

"We're all fucked."

"In that case," I turn to the waitress who had paused for us, "two whiskeys please, something Irish..." I look over the bottles, "Unavailing."

Jon smirks, "Still loving that peat."

Nodding, I drink beer, "And the women, how do they treat you here?"

"As always, as ever." He gives a hearty a belly laugh, the whiskey is delivered, the waitress smiles again at him, looks back at him as she walks away.

"Such a charmer." I say.

"Me? Ha! What about you? You're quiet moody artist schtick does you very well."

"Uh huh. Whatever you say."

"I do say so. And how are you doing with them?"

"Just fine thank you."I pause, take a breath, "I'm involved."

"Involved?" John raises his eyebrow.

"Involved."

"And."

"And what?"

"Don't be coy. Speak up, tell me about her..." He looks me over, "how you feel about her... all the juicy details."

I chuckle, sniff the scotch, take a small sip, add a tiny sprinkle of water, sip again, put it down, "She's .... fuck, she's good. She loves me, and I think I might love her."

"What's so great about her?"

"She's the first gentle thing I've known in a long time, kind to me, pretty too... I'm impressed that she still keeps that after everything she grew up ... two dads, one went bat-shit crazy religious, and her other one passed away from

cancer... been on her own in some way for a while now...
it's amazing."

John smiles at me, continuously, a small comforting smile.
"Sounds wonderful, so why do you sound so hesitant?"

"Fuck... you know... it's everything. You remember what
it was like... and sometimes, and this is the most fucked up
part, is that I miss it. I fucking miss the hanging threat of my
own god-damned death... like when you felt it, everything
was closer or realer... and I want to return to it sometimes...
but, shit, I think about ... You, remember Stephen, right? I
can't imagine doing what he did either, though. Till the very
end." I shake my head, feel heavy and weak all at once. The
whiskey smoke flavor burns as it slivers down my esophagus.

Jon nods, "Don't make it hard on yourself. It's ok to move
past it. It's ok to be happy."

"Have you?" I snap back.

John doesn't answer immediately, "I keep telling myself I
am... and I guess it works. It's better than holding on, ok.
Look, I'm not the poster boy for being fixed but I know it's a
waste to make it harder on yourself, so don't. Take it in and
be happy."

"Yep. Will do." I snort.

"Try at least," he says.

I open my mouth, pause, think, sip, "Yeah, ok." I
mumble.

It's silent. We each drink, visiting our own little versions of
hell. It's easy to develop them, something back there, kept in
the dark, like a lurking friend. Me, mine, you know. Yes,
there is everything atop that: the cold hard brute truths

about people and hate and blood and destruction… but really, that's all because of you. There, in that wild dark I sense the watcher again, see the eyes again. It's been a few months, I think. The eyes take shape, a shadowy jaguar, and it runs off.

The world materializes again around me. I feel returned, and I break the silence, "What did the Panamanians tell you about Jaguars again?" I ask, recalling an old conversation.

John blinks, looks at me, smiles, "they claimed if you wore their teeth as a necklace it would protect you from evil spirits…"

"Like the Jewish hand." I say.

"Yeah… like the hand."

"Why the teeth."

John shrugs, "Hard to get? I don't know… I knew this old abuelita once and she used to rattle on about how her husband would visit her as a jaguar at night, turn into a human and would talk to her… She told me that's how the dead came back to us, through the jaguar. Lots of people believed that, like it was a conduit thought the two worlds."

"You believe it?" I ask.

John shrugs, "I don't know, why not, stranger shit can be true, but not really… yeah, not really. What brought on these questions."

"Curious, that's all, remembering old conversations."

"What a fine time that is, something we should do again, but no longer tonight, time for me to go. I assume we'll do this again before you go?"

75

"Ok," I say. He gets up, hugs me, leaves money on the table, begins to walk out. The waitress stops him, they chat, he turns blows me a kiss and leaves.

I sit alone for a while, sipping my whiskey, feeling, trying to understand.

Outside is deep purple-black. Head is spinning, limbs warm from whiskey. City is lighted up like a parade is coming. It's not. Cold sobering me fast. Feet step lightly, as if afraid. You always have to be ready to run. Watching the night eat my breath, the small noise of each step, thinking, not thinking, walking, wanting to run. There is a small park, lonesome benches, dead shriveling trees. Like a scene from a Beckett play. Stop to look at the bench.

I'm shivering. Shivering and lost. Look around, down the road a row of pubs. Ask a drunk for directions, keep going. Some drunk girls yell out after me in a Suffolk accent. I hear them but keep walking. Thanks, but no thanks.

Make it home, at least, home for now. A narrow building bunched with other narrow buildings, my own temporary building the owner of an old stone work facade. Coming to the strange door feels perversely comforting. The key, old and heavy slides in and I'm in the foyer, a carpeted and once grandiose space, now sad and listless. Walking up the flight of stairs, reaching the sub-let. Inside the tiny minimal space now, no more than 375 sq ft.

It's all neat, organized perfectly with movement in mind. The largest luxury is a turntable with monitor speakers. Kneeling, rifling through a crate of records, I'm stopped by the silhouette of a woman's face. Reminds me of you. I put the record on. Look at the clock: 2:45 a.m. Wake up time is 6:45 a.m.

Music begins: a tender, RnB voice that reeks of longing –
a kind of existential ache to break free. Like melancholic
ecstasy. I think about wildness and devotion and Zoë. Tears
start, hot streams down my face. The record spins, the tears
continue.

Then it's done. None left. I'm sitting empty, confused.
reaching for my open bag, rifling through the contents, I find
the book she left. Open the first page. I begin to read.

The first words are a flash of lightning – unexpected,
riveting. Reading is all I have. Words for children, words
haunting, words comforting ... hitting everything like a short
range missile on target, decimating me. Tears, again.
Thinking: this is the feeling of knowing love. This is love:
crying thousands of miles away, wishing for someone.

Closing the book: the hardcover light, snapping shut.
Closing my eyes, wishing for sleep. None. There is Zoë.
There is you. Maybe more. How far it all feels. Why now?
Open doors let anyone in. Closed doors let nothing out.
Wishing now for nothing, that would be everything. But
nothing is something, and some things are too much. This,
that book, Zoë, you ... it's too much.

Finding my computer, opening it, staring at the screen,
wondering: what next? Skype opens, welcome ding, money is
in the account. Stare at the amount for a little bit of time,
then at Zoë's name. Call her. The phone rings.

RETURN TO SENDER, NO SUCH NUMBER

Time in London passes quickly in grueling routine. Some variation of studio, shoot, cocktail hour, and studio. The entourage is ever changing, models, managers, and assistants. Terry is quick to regale me with quips and cynical observations and stories of various models and designers and agents we meet, like Male model A who fell in love with a buddhist and renounced everything, only to return 2 years later as a sort-of-down low rap boy groupie with a cocaine problem. Famous names, faces, bodies and their wake of hopefuls, and hangers pollute our days. Everyone is striving, and busy ... alway busy, with busy as the focal point of self-importance.

Terry smokes reactively to all of it, relishing the carnival atmosphere, and I just listen in the background. Chatter about problems and next things and moral quandaries of banal substance. The freshest are the most naive, still filled with reverence to possibility. I like them the most. I also have no hope for them.

That feeling, of liking them, is nostalgia. I was once them ... 10 years ago, in this city. Happiness and truth and beauty were real in that space. All that was required was some cork or turn in perspective. Something, like a new place. For 3 months I wrote you everyday. Small letters. Long letters. Square letters. Oblong letters. Circular letters. Letters shaped like the void that was inside.

Such a spiritual surge, and then, nothing. No more. Just vast emptiness. Emptiness even as I traveled with my camera, seeing the beautiful and horrific. Empty even as later I walked the hollowed sacred grounds that millions fought for every day. I couldn't understand that wholesale belief everyone had, that the horizon was there. I still don't.

And now, 10 years later, in the city I first came to after you, during the small hours Terry and I have to ourselves, I amble through the streets. Sometimes with Terry, a prolix walking partner. With her, we favor the small parks that the city hides like a secret shame. Empty because of the grasping bite of a fading, but still strong, winter. The sky fluctuating from crystal blues to tender pinks and purples splotches. It rains a little, here and there; hard cold rain.

Terry tells me how she loves this weather, how she'd drink hot cocoa and read Hemingway, who her father loved. I tell her about you. Not everything, but enough, I guess. I tell her about Man-Ray, how he challenged photographic conventions, made it art. She doesn't know him. No one knows the photographer. I like that. I try to tell her more about Zoë. I can't. I feel embarrassed, I guess.

Each night, work done, I seek whiskey. Once Terry comes. That's all. I never invite her. Alone is better. After a whiskey, maybe 2, I walk. Each walk longer than the last. Only the fall of my foot, like a marching drum.

One night I am in Piccadilly Square. The lights frighten me and I slink back into the darkness. Remembering the letters I wrote you; how silly they seem... I never said anything of value: I'd write about the old couches at my

Baba's home, telling you how I'd hide behind them and listen to the adults cracking walnuts on an iron nut-cracker, the shell falling with a ding into a copper bowl. I'd remind you of the first time you had Chantilly cream. We were in Mexico and you kept ordering it, one after the other. I'd tell you about my new camera, how it worked, the grey-scale, and successful shots. Maybe you'd ask me why I wasn't painting, or why I had moved so far, or ... but it doesn't matter, because I never mailed the letters and you were gone.

Each night I walk. Each night I think these thoughts. Each night I stumble home exhausted. Before sleep, calling Zoë. Hang up, lay down, masturbate, sleep, and hope I don't dream. The only surprise was how regular my calls with Zoë had become, me finishing the day, she beginning. We expected each other.

BLESS THE TELEPHONE.

Strange
how a phone call can change your day
take you away
Away
from the feeling of being alone
Bless the telephone

The next morning. Breakfast is quick, a banana and double espresso. Head still foggy – sleep didn't come, just quiet still breaths, on my back in the dark, listening to the silences. There are many silences. In the silence, going over John's answer about Jaguars. Trying to understand the dreams I had, the feelings I have. More than a night's work, a lifetime required.

Work is at the old London docks, behemoth wood and concrete structures, the one-time keeper of the ephemera of an empire. Inside them a person feels small. Terry, the writer I'll be working with, is there, in the corner, stirring coffee looking lost. She's tall, wisp like, all wild hair and black rimmed glasses. She's proud of her glasses, old frames from her grandfather's collection. We've met before, at NYC fashion week. She was friendly, invited me to a play with her;

something by a friend. The play was loosely about relationships, but mostly about sex and alcohol. I declined.

This is the first time we'll work together. Her work tends to be sharp, sometimes it reads like satire. It's not, but, it tends toward highlighting the absurd. In fashion a lot is absurd. Same with war. Same with love. It's all absurd.

She smiles to me, waves, stops quickly, awkwardly. Now next to her, she starts to tell the itinerary.

" ... By 3:45 we'll have to meet back with the crew in an old home, somewhere in the Portobello market area, then ... 7 p.m. some kind of cocktail party, then shit, wow, she even has a midnight shoot scheduled here again... Fuck, imagine being the model, butt-ass naked at midnight in the warehouse ruins of the British Empire."

"She's relentless, eh? You meet her yet?"

"Yeah. She's a ... uhm, peculiar woman I guess. Sort of like a rabid chihuahua, but cute."

"I bet that would pass for great copy."

Terry laughs, her thin frame resembling tree branches waving in the wind.

"Anything I should be aware of?" I ask.

"Oh, yeah, she has this antagonistic relationship with photographers... like she hates them. She already fired one today... this geeky kid, for being too slow or something... I'm not sure. Anyway, she gets real particular about how things are done, and really thinks that most photographers fuck her vision up. Real clash of the titans, lady. I'm surprised she's even letting us here... first interview in years. Maybe, almost a decade."

"Ok. Yeah. Any idea why she's letting us?"

Terry laughs, "She says she likes me ... and maybe she does ... but I'm betting it's the fact that she's been on a career decline for a minute, and the Paris week is supposed to be her re-emergence with this weeks London show being the warm-up act... she's staggering the reveals, trying to be some kind of phoenix rising tale... out of the ashes and all that shit." Terry smiles like she's cataloging something, "Anyway, she wanted this profile about her done, a sort of in-depth look at the run-up of her grand re-reveal, but holy hell is she making it all sorts of complicated to be around her."

"Sure," I nod, "Why a photographer then?"

Terry shrugs, "That's the thing, she even requested you... by name and everything. She knew your work from war-zones I guess, and she's like enamored with this idea of capturing the chaos, like the middle of an explosion"

"Do you have any idea what the fuck that's actually like?" I ask, quickly and curtly.

"No..." Terry pauses, "But it sounds nice ..." Terry smiles at me, she laughs. "It's too early anyway. I'm hungover."

I let it go, "Me too. Met an old friend for drinks."

Terry nods, "I did too... except, well, I guess, he was more of an old boyfriend, or lover, is that a terrible notion? Lover, it sounds so pretentious... Anyway, it doesn't matter, we met and talked about old times and halfway through I find out he's engaged. Really dampened my mood."

"Sounds lovely."

"Even lovelier, he didn't tell me. I saw a text from his fiancé on his phone when he went to the bathroom…I didn't snoop so much as have an opportunistic glance. Really shouldn't let your texts be seen on the screen."

"A reporter through and through." I say.

"After that, I got drunk."

"And?"

"And nothing, good sir. Just stinking drunk and none of your business." Terry giggles to herself.

"I just drank with a friend, caught up, much less dramatic."

"When sex, promised or fulfilled, is involved it does tend to be decidedly more dramatic." Terry declares.

"Right. So what's the goal? What do you need from me?"

"Well, I have 5,000-ish words due, and that'll be cut as well, and you need to produce at least 8 to 12 printable shots… so whatever you want to do to accomplish that."

"Any idea of direction?" I ask

"Catch her in sordid, compromising positions." She grins.

I raise my brow.

"Ok, fine, really: human shots, her in her creative glory directing the new-line, anything that shows a proud woman grasping at the remnants of her glory."

"So simple stuff." I say.

"Yeah, mostly things where is looks like the center of the whole shit show… guiding hand and all. Quiet moments would be nice. Some stuff at the social hours would be great… she's a charming woman I hear, least when she drinks and has an audience to turn on."

"She'll be particular when you shoot her. Really intense about how she is portrayed." Terry sips her coffee, "Her assistant knows more than me, ask him, I guess…" Terry shrugs. "Look, this is her last grasp at glory. She's a living legend, and she's afraid of being put in the mausoleum while still alive."

"Fancy words." I chuckle.

"It's why they pay me the big bucks." Terry laughs. "Anyway, here's the weeks schedule. It's brutal. I mean, brutal. She's trying to prove she's still a fucking young gun. Just…" She looks me up and down, the goofy willow woman becoming something steeled and hard, "Stay sharp. That's all I need from you. Stay sharp."

I give her a smirk. "OK."

Terry, content, walks off to talk to someone, leaving the schedule in my hand. Looking it through, it's is brutal. Early morning, late nights, cocktail hours that would scream alcoholic. There is a balance to it all, as well. Very organized. It's obvious the woman is demanding.

That demanding nature comes through as the day progresses: Impossible shots expected, seams to be re-sewn in unreal time … cracked psyches, crying models, the shrill voice of the Designer still rising through it all. To me she is kind. Charming almost. Her raven black hair, perfect black jeans, white top, silver jewelry flashing at me like her smile. She's well coiffed. Easy to photograph. Still, like steal she refuses to bend to the needs and wants of others around her. Jump, march, spin, turn, do it all she explains low and calm, not to be doubted. One model is sent away after she complains it is too cold. A second steps right in, the understudy in place because being send away by our subject is quite normal. And with her iron fist she gets it done.

With Terry, later, at one of the few breaks we have. At a dim-lit dusty pub. Small, maybe 4-5 booths. The whirlwind of the day leaves me confused about our exact location. The confusion embarrasses me. Terry orders us two beers. Stouts. They arrive with a muted fan-fare.

"What do you think of our lovely lady?"

I shrug, "She's got the air of a desperate general."

"Poetic. Sounds like Hemingway." She says, considering the words, "Do you know any Hemingway?"

"The story about the fish." I say.

"So you're a learned scholar on his works then," She laughs, "he wrote this wonderful book about Paris."

I nod.

"You're not interested."

"Not really."

"OK, it doesn't matter." Terry drinks. "Personally, she's more like Earnhardt in heels."

"The race car driver?" I ask.

"Yeah, but the dad." She says.

"He has a son who races?"

"Jr."

"Family business."

"Yep."

We finish our stouts. Terry orders a second, I ask for a scotch. The waitress shoots off the choices. Glenlivet 12. She smiles at us. Asks if our honeymoon is nice. We laugh. Lovely, Terry says. I don't say anything.

"It's good to know we seem familiar." Terry says.

"Yep."

Terry looks at me. She contemplates something, "The woman is so driven, I mean, like she's trying to smash everything in her way. Like Earnhardt." Terry gives herself a smile.

"You like Nascar then?"

"Oh," She trails off, thinks, "Well, sort of? I dunno. An old boyfriend showed it to me...and I sort of like it." Terry frowns. The explanation seems dull to her.

"Seems sort of repetitive," I say.

Terry thinks, "Yea ... it is ... the attraction is more ... uhm, it's sort of more about the crashing. Or the potential to crash. The danger I guess," Terry stops, continues, "It sounds weird ok, but I like the potential of crashes. It seems so reckless and it sort of makes me feel ... just anything really. To do it you need this really pure focus, just pure drive."

"Is that literally or metaphorically?" I ask.

Terry laughs, "Both, I guess."

"I get it. It's how you know you're living."

"Right." Terry drinks, her tone is wistful, "So the boyfriend left, or something, and I still watched Nascar, even though I thought I hated it."

"He left you a souvenir of his time."

"Yeah, I guess he did. Anyone leave you a souvenir?" Terry asks.

"I don't know. Maybe?"

"Don't ask me. I wouldn't know." Terry sours.

"No, I guess you wouldn't."

"Do you know?"

"About myself?"

"Yes, you ass."

No response. Souvenirs? No, nothing from the gift shop. But that's not the question, and it's not what I meant. I know what I meant. I don't care for the answer. If there is one, if there might be one; I don't care.

"No. I don't think so." I say.

Terry drinks, "Suit yourself." She shrugs. There is a lull, "Seeing anyone?"

"Yeah. I think I am." I say.

Terry brightens, "What's she like?"

"She's..." I stop and consider Zoë — consider her meandering phrases, her particular tastes, and "She's kind to me Really fucking kind. Beautiful, too. And I'm uncomfortable with it. Feels really odd."

Terry shakes her head. "Don't be an idiot, ok. Just don't be an idiot. Someone gives you that, don't be an idiot. You think about it too much you'll just think yourself into a mistake. Don't do that."

"I think my problem is a lack of thinking."

"Right, so don't do that either. Don't do what I do, and don't do what you do."

"That's broad and unclear." I say

"Sure, but still, don't do any of it.

"I'll try not to." I say. I smile. The first smile for Terry in London.

Look at the clocks. Time to move. Pay the bill. Smile again, this for the waitress. A lovely, lovely honeymoon.

A party next. Fine dressed folks. I dive into the background. Observe. There is an art-like elegance to the proceedings. Many models. Designers. Politicians smattered about. Money-traders, as well. Rich and famous, and the requisite groupies.

Mental chess-matches unfold before me. Everyone trying to understand the leverage the next person is capable of giving them. Sex, or, money, or position, or power. All mingling and interchangeable.

Terry finds me occasionally. She asks for a photograph, so and so speaking. As she asks, she fills me in on the minor intrigues. The failing marriage, the coke-habit becoming addiction, the quiet alcoholic. I nod, ignore most of it. Their own business is their own business... I just point and shoot.

Behind the camera I'm invisible. People don't believe I can see. Fine by me. It's merely human nature unfolding. Like the animal kingdom, little games for power and control. Each winner, at once losing, each loser soon to be winner. Circling the room and it's all the same. No real conversation. The designer Terry and I are here for, floating through, trying to milk the crowd for whatever good will the party bought her. Flatter the models, convince them that stardom is here. Flatter the politicos, convince them that their presence matters. Flatter the rich, convince them they are loved by the rest, those others. She is an expert, and it makes some sense.

You would hate this event and it's family. I know how sincere and forward you were. I remember that well. I miss it. How calmly and beautifully you would tell me: "I don't want pretend. Pretend isn't interesting. I want real things. Real me and real you."

Real me isn't ok. Real me is not ready for any of this. No, what matters is getting each shot right and moving on. Keep moving on, even as I can't.

The night ends slowly, in a lingering fashion. Terry lets me know I can leave when all that remains are a young actor, 3 or 4 models, and a diplomat. Even our host, the women we are slated to follow, has disappeared to rest.

I ask Terry if she wants company home. She shoos me off, says she is staying, invites me. I say no.

Outside, it's supposed to be a full moon. Can't tell, too much light pollution. The city feels empty. Google maps tell me I have only 3 miles to walk, or a 14 quid cab ride. I choose to walk. I don't know the streets. The unfamiliarity comforts me. So little comforts me.

Thinking about you comforts me. It upsets me, too. In the field, where danger was live, I wasn't upset. There was no time for that. The worst nights weren't the live ones. The worst were the quiet ones, in the confines of safety. Then it's the quiet fears that come for you. I recall nights like those in cities like this across the world. Safe nights.

Those nights are the nights I swear I'll unravel. I didn't and I don't and I won't. It's the feeling of you that lingers, the feeling you imbued me with and I still long for.

In foreign streets it's easier. Nothing to remind me. No triggers of the long conversations we once shared. Do you remember that night when I had to find you? You were so angry, and you had gone to the Israeli cafe, 6 miles from home. You had a cup of coffee in front of you and you didn't drink coffee. Maybe that's what struck me about Zoë holding that cup. Maybe. Or maybe I miss you. That conversation, that night, was so beautiful. They closed the cafe around us. The young Israeli's who worked there talking to us so kindly. I was content to let you talk. By the end you weren't angry at all.

What were you angry about? Do you remember? I don't. I remember how weary you looked. Smiling just a little, tired, a little sheepish.

"I guess I wasn't so composed, was I?" You asked me, as we walked home together.

Of course you were. Always were. You'd say I'm not giving it an honest look. Faults and crack-lines, everyone has them. We are all broken. Life is learning that being broken is ok.

I'm broken. It's ok.

But I don't believe it.

Standing still, smelling the light rain on the concrete. Three cigarette smokers speak near by about a soccer match. I listen. Try to. Their terms are slurred and strange, so I stop. The rhythms of their words carry me. It's like a bastardized waltz.

I drift to my temporary home, thinking: someone loves me, I love her. I hope. I love you, I know. God-damn, I know so little. So ignorant.

Inside now, my tiny refuge. I find a record, Astrud Gilberto. Listening, that subtle voice, that tenderness. As Astrud sings to me, I read. The words are music. The cadence enchanting. Astrud and Antoine.

The laptop open, the ditty of Skype, and Zoë's name first in line. It's afternoon for her. The ring of the phone.

Her mellifluous voice answering: "I miss you." She coos, I can hear the smile.

Smiling now too, "You know, I'm ok with you." I say.

"Just ok?" She teases.

"No, that's not exactly..." She waits patiently for my words, I try and find them, "With you I feel ok with myself."

Her tongue clucks, a little sign that she is pleased, "That's a good thing," She assures.

Silence now, spreading warmth; silence like a warm night and cool breeze and midnight with a full moon.

"You know I love you." She tells me.

I'll tell you too. "Wonderful." I say.

No demands for a return of the phrase. Hoping she hears it in my voice. Whispers in my head, I love you, over and over again. To her. To you. One day, to me.

She talks on. I ask questions just to listen. Then she must go.

"I love you." I whisper. I don't know if she hears me.

THEY SAY DROWNING IS THE EASIEST WAY TO GO.

My last night in London, before onward to Paris, I meet John for drinks in a smug-evil wooden pub.

"I'm starting to understand that cliché about distance and fondness and hearts." I say.

Johns raises an eyebrow, "Really... How so?" He cocks an asymmetrical smile.

"Don't play stupid, you know how so, the clue is the fucking phrase." I say.

"Ok... so, what are you going to do then?"

"Do?"

"Yes, do. As in: you're all doe-eyed smitten and she seems to be to ... so what will you do with that information?"

"Nothing. I mean, I don't know, ok?" I stammer. "Anyway, it's not like it has to mean anything ... it's not ... it's just, fuck, you know, something."

"Most people have relationships." John says.

"Right." I say.

"Maybe she likes how clueless you are. It's cute, in a way."
John says.

"What would you do?"

"If I loved someone?"

"Yes." I answer.

"I'm not an expert, but in the past: I dated her, I moved in
with her, we worked, then we didn't … She left me. I got
sad. Its very simple Boy meets Girl stuff here. Come on,
Jaleel, you must have better sense than this. Didn't you live
with someone one once."

"Yeah … I have…the last person I lived with, she was just
as off as me, I guess. She did photo-work on the sex trade
and that stuff really fucked with her head. We lived in New
York and saw each other maybe a third of the time… the
whole arrangement was closer to comrades in war, just with
sex."

"See, you have an example right there…"

"Yeah … but … we … Look, we lived across the way
from the hospital and the sirens were this weird little lullaby
for us, like our song. And it worked because we sort of knew
we were just place holders, like the hospital across the way,
and once we were better we'd check out. We both
understood that and it was ok."

John shakes his head, smiles, "Jesus fuck man. Look, it's
hard, right? Love… and it doesn't get easier, but it's worth it,

and the only way to find out if it can work is if you invest in it. For real, a real invest of yourself. And even if you do that, be ok if it fails, because it does most of the time anyway."

His words sink, heavy. Pondering them, finally, I say: "I can't."

"Why not?"

A shrug, "Too frail I guess."

"Fuck you." John snarls. "We all are. All of us. But you know better than most how resilient people are. You've seen them … you used to work with them everyday… people who should have given up long ago and let the world fuck them, and still get up and keep going. These are people suffering because some man in a mansion wants more gold faucets, and more silk, and more woman, and he needs more oil and minerals for that, and they keep going still. Do you get that? They keep going. So keep going. Don't tell me shit." John deflates, "Just feel something, let it happen; asshole. You won't wither and die if you do."

"I'm trying." I say.

"Are you really?" John asks.

Nothing from me.

"You know I love you, you're a good friend most of the time… but … ah, fuck it, just try, just try to let it happen."

"Thanks." I say.

The rest of the night we drink to milder conversations — his school work, the characters we've met in the past, his current lovers, two of them, a French woman with a temper, and a Japanese woman with a taste for vodka.

I leave him, drunk, and tonight I don't walk the city. Straight home. I play a record: Haydn, piano sonata 4. You loved the tinkling melody.

I try and think. Then I try and feel. Then I fall into a half haze sleep. Now I dream. In the room with me is the jaguar, sinewy and wild. Close in I can see the sheen of his coat, the faint patterns of black on black. The jaguar is calm, unperturbed at finding itself perched atop a fake wood bookshelf in a tiny flat in London. The jaguar looks serene, in fact. I am not. Sweat pours from me.

We stare at one another ... primeval feelings. So much fear in me.

I tell myself: it's a dream. It will go away.

The past arises now. Everything, the images of anger and destruction and greed and the failure of humans ... there are bitter words in song, loneliness of prisoners, emptiness of children's bellies — distended like bridges of hopelessness... the burning sun over the refugee camps of Libya and Sudan, tents over what was once forested land thousands of years before, now a wasteland where humans are shunted to rot... the clear cutting in Panama again, the moveable peasant making temporary homes in the shadow of the forest. Images coming one atop the other, bleeding together. I'm crying. It's too damn much. Put them away in a camera. Don't let it eat you.

"What do you want!" I shout, start to mumble, "take it and go ... take it and go... " over and over.

No answer, just the unbroken stare of hazel gold-green eyes, eyes like Zoë's.

Calm quiet returns. Breathing deeply, inhale, exhale.

The Jaguar remains, watching me.

The past recreates itself, revealing to me:

Meeting you, the anticipation, the release. Day spent at the beach, pretending to build sand castles, sand shifting from our hands back to the shore. Holding the tips of your fingers in mine the first time they touched snow... warming them.

The more recent past reveals itself to me:

Zoë is prominent — her sharp chin, thin lips, small ears, and half cocked smile, beguiling me. The night she cooked for me ... and never did again, and she laughed as we colored like children. The hike we took, as she counted the trees, and we jumped into the cold river with hysterics.

The Jaguar remains, watching me.

My hallucinatory descent; as I'm pleading still, take it and go... take it and go... take it and go... like a sing-song mantra now. I want clarity. I want understanding.

None forthcoming.

The Jaguar remains, watching me.

The pumping of my heart gives me the rhythm in which the blood and fluids dance through the arterial connections. Following the beat, I feel weightless. Looking at the Jaguar, now, as if from above. The Jaguar's obsidian colored coat expands, swallowing everything. The sheen blackness curls into a wave below me... it grows and gains speed, coming on fast. The wave crashes atop me... I go under. I flail, trying to hold on, stay afloat. Suspended now in darkness.

The breath tightens. The pressure increases. The breath tightens. The pressure increases.

GOING WEST

Terry is bouncing beside me, our luggage piled at our feet, as the train slows to a halt in front of us.

" That shit cray ... that shit cray... that shit cray ... that shit cray ... Pa'ri' ... Pa'ri' ... Par'ri'." Terry chants, matching the popular songs melody.

"That all you know?" I ask.

She looks at me, bobs her head, smiles wryly, "Don't let me get in my zone ... Don't let me into my zone ...Don't me into my zone ... the stars is in the building, they hands is to the ceiling... I know I'm bout to kill, how you know? I feel it."

I laugh at her, "Excited?"

"No, no, not at all." Terry shakes her head empathetically, "not for Paris, Paris... this shit cray..." she begins again.

Letting her finish, ushering us onto the train, finding our seats, settling in, "What's the attraction?" I ask, as we sit.

"Of Paris?" She asks.

"No, the song." I say.

"Well, probably the outsized melody.. I mean, that shit cray."

"Uh huh, and Paris, what about Paris?" I say.

"Oh, Pairs…" She sounds wistful. "Yes, well, Ernest, and James, and Gertrude, and Coleridge, and Elliot, and Ezra, and Francis, and Zelda … oh, yes…"

"Friends?" I ask.

Terry laughs, "The best."

"Ok." I say, confused.

"Writers, from the 20's and 30's Jazz Age," Terry answers my confusion. "A lot of them moved to the left bank after WW1." She finishes explaining.

"That's the draw for you?" I ask.

She nods at me, turns to the little blonde Scandinavian girl standing close to her mother just 5 feet away, starts making faces at her, "Yes, literature and lattes."

"Sounds idyllic. A little too romantic for my tastes." I say.

"It is romantic, super romantic." Terry says, squeaking as the train arrives.

Shuffling through the kerfuffle of passengers, settling into seats with a table between us, facing each other.

Terry picks the thread up once more, "It's silly, sure, I know that... but I need shit like that, ok? I mean don't you? Something make-believe, a little sum-thang sum-thang to cheer up the shit we dredge through?"

I shrug.

"Jesus, really? I mean like, hey maybe there I get inspired again, write for myself again, maybe all I get is a fuck with French man who likes to read poems to me while I take a bath..."

I laugh.

"What's funny?"

"Not much... the image of you bathing getting read to by a man smoking a cigarette with a bun in his hair."

"Don't invade my fantasies, pervert."

"Ok, sorry."

"But you don't feel that at least? A little bit? Some need for escape?" She pleads a little for understanding.

"Escape? Yeah, I get that." I really do. I've been looking for escapes the whole time. Escape the dreams. Escape you.

My response exasperates Terry; she wanted something more visceral, "Fine, maybe you're just sad then? You don't get to have your friend with you... what's her name?"

"Zoë." I say. Yes, I am sad she's not here.

"Right, Virgin of Christ and all, sorry I'm bad with names." Terry says, "So?"

"So what?"

"Do you want her to here? With you?" She asks. Feels like middle school, when a friend of a friend asks for a friend if you like so and so.

Well, I do like so and so, "I ..." want to say yes, cause I want her here, "It's complicated." I say instead.

"Complicated? It's not a fucking Facebook status." She shrieks at me.

"It is."

"What? What is so fucking complicated?"

I shrug.

"You sound like a moody little teenager." She says, "Ok, fine I get it, I'm prying. Can't really blame me, I am a journalist, after all."

Terry stretches herself out as she finishes speaking, laying on her back and disappearing from view, her legs which hung in the aisle lift into the air above her as she kicks one foot straight then the other, her ballet flats like a propeller through the air. Her hair is all I can really see from my vantage point, it's thin black strands spreading out over the seat looking like roots of a new seedling. And I think about nutrients again. About growth, about imperfection, about what stays and what leaves us, about Zoë.

LEFT BANK FEASTS

We reach Paris at dusk. Rain and rich grey skies, like Seattle's, welcome us. Terry and I bumble through enough French to get a taxi to the hotel, a chic-modern boutique across from the Square Émile-Chautemps. The lobby is bright, cheery and cheeky, with true white walls and fire engine red accents. Each of our rooms is themed, mine is minimalist modern in black and white. Terry's room, the floor above mine, looks like a 1950's romance film, a place for Lauren Bacall to weep and rejoice in. Dropping stuff off we eat at the hotel cafe. Parting back to our rooms, hoping to sleep.

After an hour of lying still, trying to rest, a knock on my door. I put on pants. At the door is Terry.

"It's late," I say, opening the door, letting her through.

"I can't sleep for shit," She's already on the tiny balcony smoking a cigarette.

"Neither can I."

"Get drunk?" She asks.

"Sure, enough to sleep, at least," I say.

We head down. The concierge directs us to a bar. It's 3 blocks away, just around the Square. The night is cold, but spring is anticipating. Finding the location, slipping inside, sitting at a flimsy table. Creole jazz music is playing. Terry orders an absinthe. I order Port. We drink. Terry despises the absinthe.

"Why order it?" I ask.

"Books..." She says, while ordering a wine.

After the second drink, as the third arrives, Terry starts delicately, "I have to ask again..."

"So ask." I say.

"Do you, I mean, not in a body way, but in a real sort of feel it down inside way, miss your woman friend at home?"

"Woman-Friend? We're not 80." I say, taking a quaff.

"Oh fuck off it, you know what I mean."

I sigh, "I do. I do miss her."

There is a long space, we both drink.

"So why not just say that outright?"

I don't answer quickly. Terry is right. Why don't I answer simply? There is you, of course, but I don't have to say anything about you. Then there is me, admitting to myself ... as if it's a mistake and mistakes hurt. "Maybe I'm just confused." I say to Terry.

Terry is satisfied with this answer, "We all are anyway."

We order one more drink each. Order food as well; olives, a goat cheese tart, a panna cotta. Terry tells me about the history of the left bank, of the artist, of the little bookshop, James Joyce going blind, his dirty letters; Fitzgerald and the wild marriage he had that leaked alcohol at the seams, Hemingway and his temper; Coleridge, his opium and sunless seas, and Pound who watched his stash; Stein, her cruelty and her bravery and her benevolence...

I listen intently. Somehow the past feels more alive. Everyone else's pain for me to consume, never my own.

Terry's speech slows down, she's talked herself out and if we drink more we'll be drunk. Paying, leaving, shivering to our temporary home. Good night all around, see you in the morning. My door shuts behind me.

Inspired, believing I can tell you simply and outright. Pen, paper, desk! Collect my thoughts and send them off...

Words begin to follow, slow and laborious, but they come. A time later and 2 letters: one to you, one to Zoë.

To you, I write:
Each day is hard since you left. It never gets easier, but I guess it's not supposed to. I imagine us siting together again sometimes, 2 glasses of mint julep, chatting. Nothing in particular, I guess, it'd be enough to hear your voice. Someday I imagine I see you, in the corner of these parties I attend, or walking the street; but that's a trick of the eye. I love you still. That will never change. Do you love me? I'm really trying to move on, I'm doing my best to leave it behind me. Like you said to me all the time: I can't go on, I will go on.
  Love
  Jaleel

To Zoë, I write:

I'm still surprised at the depth of your kindness. It's frightening and refreshing. There are words I wish I knew how to say, actions I wish I knew where to begin. Thoughts of you comfort me — your silly games and gentle demeanor... Why you find me worthwhile baffles me, but I'll keep trying. I'll be my best.

Love

Jaleel.

I put each letter into an envelope, seal them, address them, and retire to bed. I dream of the jaguar again. The black coat, the golden eyes watching me still. The next morning I ask the front desk to ensure the letters are mailed.

ONE FOOT IN FRONT OF THE OTHER.

The next week in Paris and everything is a haze. There is wine, Terry continuing the inter-related histories of the left-bank artists — the Lost Generation — as Stein called them … their amoral lives. It's a nice juxtaposition, models, parties, drink and drugs, soundtracked by the dead artists revived in Terry's easier imagination. Surrounded by tabloid fodder, headline names, whispers of who and what; and Terry is immersed in detailing Ernest and Hadley, their marriage shattered by that harpy Pauline and all the alcohol everyone drank.

Terry's history lessons are a welcome relief; the work is easy enough now. Anticipating our subjects moods and movements became easy as soon as I start to think of her as a dictator. Her shrill demands and abrupt turn face to sweetness just a master class in narcissism, not greatness, but control. That's all power is, control. Taking and bending your environment to suit your own needs. What does our subject need? Adoration and the feeling of being an iconoclast… when given that she is easy to shoot. When she is not? I disappear for a spell. Walk the city. Let it die down, let her need me to return; feel the need to charm my camera again.

By the last 2 days I am hardly needed. There is only her social hours and her interviews to be present for. I walk a lot. The last of winter dying out, spring trying. It's time of revival and renewal. Open the windows and breathe again, the ground fertile and fecund. The city starting to come alive again, singles out and prowling... the past summer lovers become autumn become winter becoming restless with the summer again, starting to wonder if they should stay or go. Sideways glances and hope that this year will bring something fresh, like every spring ... And I'm going home to see what the summer before meant, what dancing is, and what sharing histories might mean, and if I really can accept, let go, and walk away from everything before.

IT'S SAID WE NEVER FORGET HOW TO RIDE A BICYCLE.

Seattle's skyline, settled against the Puget sound, rises on the north horizon as Zoë drives us into the city from SeaTac. It's a crisp March day, touched by a weak sun.

"It was raining for days before you arrived" Zoë tells me.

"It's nice to see the sun," I say, "I saw very little of it."

Zoë smiles, "I'm happy you're back."

"Thanks… it feels nice," I only rally a wan smile in return.

"Do you want to go anywhere? Need food or tea?" Zoë asks, her right hand reaching out toward mine.

I look at her waiting hand, resting in the center console. Lazily I rest mine atop hers, slump into my seat, and close my eyes. In my palm I can feel her warmth, my fingertips wrapping to feel her raised knuckles across the back of her hand. Zoë, I missed her, like all hell. I'm relieved to be back, to be home.

But.

But I still feel an unclear tension, a gnawing fear like a skittish animal. I'll call it jet lag for now.

"No, nowhere... just home. I could nap." I say.

"Anything you want," She says.

Anything. What do I want?

THE WEATHER HAS ITS OWN
AGENDA

Life's routine — Zoë, work, self-maintenance — returns quietly. More and more I gain a sense of comfort. Three weeks after I've returned an email upends that feeling. A representative from Whitesmith Gallery in downtown writes, asking for more of my portfolio, and about dates for a show, whether or not I'd do press. Confused, I call. A chipper young voice, talking in machine gun sentences, informs me that everyone is excited to work with me, and my work is haunting, but so good. I hang up, more confused, but armed with the coordinator's cellular. Her name is Anne Teimme.

Another weeks passes before the mystery is solved. Sean calls me, asks why I've not reached out to Anne.

"Who?" I ask.

"Anne, from Whitesmith." Sean says.

"I don't feel like it." I pause, "How the fuck do you know about that?" I'm hostile.

"She's a friend of mine." He says.

"Friend?" I ask.

"Yeah…"

"Look, Sean, I'm not sure what's going on… but, I'm not into the idea."

"Meet her, at least, J." Sean implores.

"What's in it for you?" I ask.

"Nothing." He says.

"Look, she liked your photos she saw hanging at mine. Asked to borrow them. I let her borrow them and gave them your contact. She's their main coordinator for shows, J. Biggest gallery in the Northwest."

"You let her borrow pieces? What the fuck does that even mean?" I ask.

"Just meet her."

"Whatever, fine." I mumble. I don't intend to call.

In total he had lent her 13 pieces. I'd only given him 9. The last 4 are a mystery to me.

SOMETIMES OK IS ENOUGH.

Lunch hour rush is dying down; from the window at Fonte where I wait I can see the rain-jacketed people dash about. Spring is in full effect, heavy drops of warming rain falling like a blanket today. Coffee arrives, absently I drink. I wait for Sean. He is to arrive in 15 minutes. I'm early to compose myself, gather my thoughts.

A copy of the NY Times rest beside me. Most of the news is vaguely familiar. Same story, told again and again: People in need. People in excess. Ideas in conflict. Resources coveted and fought for. War. Famine. Rape. It's all civilization unfolding. The animals and the zookeeper or some such saying.

Sighing, pushing the paper away, closing my eyes. The news is too much on an empty stomach. Anyway, I learned Stalin was right: tragedies as statistics. In time, even your own tragedies become the average, like statistics.

Sean taps my shoulder. I open my eyes, look at him. He sits beside me, orders a coffee. I ask for more cream. I don't say anything, content to examine him: his light coppery skin showing the first encroaching signs of aging and stress at the edges, there his ever present smile — not welcoming, but warning — and the quick eyes that seem to study all the peripherals.

"She fuck you well?" I snark.

"Like hell, like good time hell. Artsy chicks, man, artsy chicks are like a whole 'nother level up." Sean says.

"Great." I mumble.

His coffee arrives. He prepares it. I glare at this hands, working to perfect his caffeine intake. The moment is bruised.

"Why don't you talk to her?" Sean asks, exasperated.

"Why the fuck does she have my work in the first place?" I snarl.

"Cause you gave them to me, and I hung them, and she liked them, begged for them, and this is good for you ... J, she runs the nicest gallery in the city. You can sell that stuff, you can make a name... I ... Jesus, Jaleel, it's an opportunity."

"Who the hell made you made me my agent?"

"Well you don't do it for yourself."

"No. I don't. And it's not your damn business is it?"

"It is my damn business. I made it my damn business. Those were good pieces. I like them, and you have a chance..."

"Fuck you." I cut him off.

"No, fuck you. Take some help for once. I'm helping you out." He implores.

"You don't know what you're doing then." I say.

"J, I've known you for… years, almost 20, and, I … just, damn-it man, I'm trying to be helpful. Take that for once, take someone's help."

"So I can be like you?"

"I told you I like my life. I enjoy what I do, whom I fuck, the money I make. I like it." He growls.

No words follow. We glare at each other, at the shop, at the public passing by. He likes his life, great, I think. It's his choice. But to force it on me? Force what? A chance at things being different. At displaying my work. That hurts. What hurts? All of this short term life. Everything just meant to be wasted, like you Sean, and you Zoë.

"Ok." I say.

"Ok?" Sean asks.

"Ok."

"Need more clarity than that, ok what?"

"I'll talk to her. I'll make an effort, an honest one."

Sean relaxes, "Really?"

"Yea, I'll try." I say.

"Wow. Ok, alright." He drinks coffee, nods, smiles, and "Ok."

The rain continues, but it looks nurturing, like it means to give something.

"Well, shit." He says, sighs, and sips his coffee.

SHE'S NO RAGGITTY ANNE

A week later. At Bauhaus Coffee, north of downtown. Waiting, again. Students occupy every square inch, crowding in the many corners the shop has from its unorthodox shape. Studious and lazy, all at once. Books surround them, waiting in the library built into the walls behind them, stacked on their tables around them like a child's fort. Anne is expected in an hour. This leaves me time to settle. Be still. The door is in my direct line of sight from where I sit.

On the start of the second coffee cup, about a half hour in, the stillness starts. Breath slows, the outside fades, becomes distant noise. All thinking ceases. Once, at a Buddhist retreat I attend, when I came home after photographing my first war, they told me this was meditation. I suppose it is. I don't care. It's protection, I told them. Erasing myself in the moment — because pain only hurts the individual. There was, is, too much. I left the retreat. Left the woman who took me. I didn't want their freedom of escape. Not then at least. Now, now I do.

Last night a dream plagued me. I woke confused, drenched in sweat, feeling the adrenaline in me. Zoë woke with me. Startled, wide-eyed, afraid, Zoë. She came to me, soothing rubs to my back, gentle flourishes on my spine. My body shaking, she asking: What's wrong. No answer — none known to give. Her fingers on my neck, lips graceful on my forehead. I should tell her. Tell her what? I'll tell you, if you'd come back. I'll tell you, not her, you, then you keep my secret, my burden. Protect it, far away from here. I'll tell you. Not Zoë, no, I can't tell her.

In the darkness, her mouth attempting to comfort me; with words, with soft brushes. Her body warm, my own cold. She envelopes me, her soft tender womanhood embraces me, engulfs me, rocks me softly to sleep like a lullaby. When I woke this morning, for the first in a long time, the world felt kind. At breakfast, Zoë wishes me luck with such a simple, genuine smile.

Well, Zoë, let's test your wish. Anne is arrived, sitting in front of me, smile like a shark, black sheen hair, pale skin, large yellowish-blue eyes. She sips at a cappuccino, offering a Latte to me.

"Sean told me you like them," She explains.

I do.

"It's very nice to meet you." Anne says, after I accept her offering.

I nod, sure, pleasure, all pleasure.

"You're a genius with the camera," She gushes, shark smile.

"No, just there, at the right time and circumstance." I counter.

Shark smile still, "There is a genius to that."

"No, it's not, ok? I mean, those things... you pay for them? That's how it gets done, you pay for it somehow." I say.

Her smile slips away, her demeanor chess-like, considering, and slowly she nods, "I understand, I can empathize that it's not easy.."

Silent. Anne, you don't understand; I think: You want something provocative, something intense, something to incite and titillate. That you understand. Damn it, Anne, I'm going to give it to you. For many reasons: I feel lost and confused, I need to put it away and maybe if people it buy it, they buy what it cost me to get it, and because of Zoë. Because I love her and want to try, ok? I can make it this time. (Zoë, what do you see in me? Tell me the secret, whisper it to me that little big secret like the breath of life) I have faith. Or, at least, someone has faith in me, and that may just be enough.

"Look, cut the act, you don't need to inflate me or soothe me, ok? I'm going to work with you." I say.

Anne gives a tight smile, but her eyes open wide and hungry, with a quick change to business demeanor, she asks, "How much more photos like those do you have? I mean that's not owned or catalogued by your old employers."

"A lot." I say. And good riddance. Keep them all, Anne, keep them. Perfect encapsulations of whatever you are looking for: chaos unfiltered, evocative portraits of life that prove God is a cruel taskmaster. Except, don't be fooled Anne, there is no God there, not there nor here. Just people, shitty people and their shitty ways; all captured in poignant ways with the right balance of Aperture and F-stop and stored on a digital file.

Anne is triumphant, and she continues, "The gallery will of course handle ...," a slate of words she learned at a marketing course, the directional creative philosophy of so and so, and so and so ... the last detail will be managed perfectly. For this, I have faith in Anne. "We pride ourselves on making the experience a pleasure for the artist." She concludes.

A true pleasure, for a new and true artist. In front of me are the contracts, drawn up by the snap legal team. Here is my percentage, standard of course for an unknown, and more than other galleries... all we need is my signature here and here. Send them to us once you've reviewed them.

Have them, Anne, take them and leave me.

Then just a few last minute details: expected delivery date, obligations for the opening push, and a bio, if I could send it over when I have the time.

A bio? A bio: Me; a tiny of fraction infinity, adrift, not born, rather appearing from some forgotten misted morn... how's that?

Awkward Anne, as she's gathering her triumph, "Maybe work on it a bit?" She suggest.

Sure, Anne, Sure.

THE RARE SILVER VULPES VULPES

The evening at Zoë's is uneasy. Nothing settles me, hash, whiskey, a warm bath, some pages from a novel, and I'm pacing still. Zoë heats us dinner in the kitchen — a lentil and sausage stew. I step into the kitchen and watch her. Domestic bliss. It's an odd sensation. I'm still adjusting, learning to appreciate the quiet.

"Can you chop the kale into ribbons?" Zoë asks me.

Grabbing a cutting board, a nice knife, I slice the kale. When she asks I put it into the stew. Together we watch the kale start to soften into the stew. I turn the stove heat down to the lowest setting. Zoë gets bowls and utensils, sets the table.

We sit, cheerily she eats, "I got this from a farmers market near UW," she tells me.

"What were you doing there?" I ask.

"At the library reading about nueroplasticity and also about kangaroos."

"Different topics." I say.

"Uh-huh," She smiles, eats, "The kangaroo uses it's pouch to hold the new born, which is like jelly bean sized and has to slither itself to the pouch from vagina."

"Gross."

"It's awesome." Zoë laughs.

"Learn anything else?"

"Well…" She pauses, eats, "I was reading about how the brain is able to learn and grow still, that it's not something stagnant." She says.

"What's that mean?"

"Your neural pathways change from your environment and behavior patterns and even what you feel or go through, both physically and emotionally."

"Sounds reasonable."

"Right, and for a long time it was thought that those pathways can't change… but it seems they do. It could be a huge for …" She takes a lingering second to look at me, "people with trauma, or injuries, it's a hope that they can develop new patterns and ways of looking at the world that are healthier. The brain and body can learn to be something new."

Thinking about change. It's possible, available. "That sounds nice," I say.

Zoë nods, kisses me, looks at my bowl, "Is that all you're eating?"

"I can't eat more." I say. My bowl is only half consumed.

Zoë frowns, takes the food and begins to clean the kitchen.

Watching her is pleasant. Almost inspiring. Standing behind her, gripping her hips, kissing her lower neck, "I'm going to chop wood," I say.

The woodpile is outside, in a little grove of tall skinny pines, covered by a tarp. It's raining lightly. The earth below my feet is soft. I pile a section of wood, place one on a chopping stump. Ax in hand, smooth birch handle, about 2 1/2 feet long. Strong steel blade. Step back, left hand at the ax handle base, bringing it above my head, catching the mid handle with my right, swinging it back around in a single smooth motion. The steel head cracks into the wood, the wood splinters. Loosening the head from the indentation. One smooth motion, again, cracking the wood deeper. Switching the base hand to the right now. 2 strokes. Switching the base hand again. The thick wood piece breaks. I break it further down. Chop 4 more pieces similarly. A large bundle done, placing it onto my forearms, carrying it inside.

Stacking it by the fireplace, Zoë lifts her head from reading, smiles at me. I return outside. Chop more. The motion is soothing and rhythmic when done right. Zoë is outside now, watching me. I stop.

"I think we have enough wood," She says.

"I like this." I say.

"Well, come inside, it's nice, start the fire." She turns and goes back in.

"Ok." I say, chopping 2 more large pieces.

Back inside the spacious living room, sitting at the front of the fireplace. The wood is laid out in a pattern to catch, kindling below the pieces. The fresh cut wood, damp from rain, is placed beside the fire grate where it can dry.

"Make it small, it's late." Zoë says.

"I'm awake," I start the kindling.

She shrugs, returns to reading. She finishes a page and sets the book aside. She watches me.

"I feel like prey." I say

"Oh?"

"Yeah, and your a sly fox hunting me."

She laughs, a light, nearly cruel, laugh, "I'd hunt you so cleverly... and look so nice doing it." Her vanity touched, she preens herself.

"You like being a fox?"

A laugh again, "I'm going to get you."

"You're an odd one." I say.

She slinks down from the chair, crawls quietly too me, pretending to be a fox. Beside me, she nuzzles into my neck. Her long dark hair covers my shoulders. She coos, then sighs.

The flames grow as the larger logs catch. One of the logs hisses and cracks as water begins to escape.

Her head lolls, slipping down ward, and comes to rest on my thigh, her hair covering my knees now. The back of her head digs into my thigh and she stretches herself, fox like; she's soft, content, and with every slight movement the tendrils of her hair brush me. My hands pet her, soothing her as I can, soothing me in the recess of an emotional self not visited often. A place nearly forgotten: the scent of cloves in black tea, the sound of cracking walnuts backed by the chorus of your laughter. Your laughter, my laughter, everyone laughing... the quiet nights with you alone ... the pleasantness of being... the softness of the sea, sand running through my cupped fingers as if an hourglass ... diving into the sea, the rocky reefs, the creatures that adapt: soft anemone, hard-looking urchins, sly octopi, all hiding and darting in the delicate corals...

Dive deeper still. Find more. Find me. Finding endless caves, peering into them, trying to see, but only greeted by obsidian darkness, like a veil. Hearing songs in the submergence: Come away with me, come away with me ... Look at where we are, remember where we started out, when it sings will you know my name?

Growing wildly, Growing alone. Finding you. Losing you. I'm always coming back home, never free to let you go, this pain of you.

My pain.

We all have aches and pains.

Aches and pains...

Aches and pains ...

To solve it Langston Hughes suggested asking the river for a kiss. Sylvia Plath had her head in over for bliss. Hemingway and Thompson met shotgun shells when the bell came tolling.

Gone from the aches and pains.

Damn it, damn them, damn this, I'm here, on a soft carpeted floor, holding a beautiful woman, so damned beautiful in so many lights. She loves me, loves me wonderfully with never wavering green-hazel eyes.

For the first time since you left I feel like I have a chance that's not you. It's hope, nothing grand, but something. Something, I hope.

HABITATION RESTORATION

There is the faint scent on pines in the morning, wafting in from the open window. A bright wonderful morning. Clear. Zoë sleeps soundly, smiling faintly. I hum a tender melody, kiss her forehead, slip out of bed and dress quietly.

In the kitchen I prepare coffee in the French press, starting with the fragrant grounds, adding a splash of vanilla extract, — made by Zoë from bourbon, vodka, and used beans — maple syrup, and pinches of cinnamon. The water muddles the mix as it cascades into the vessel. The recipe is something Zoë learned from her father Jean. After 5 minutes I stir the muddy water, it dances. I let it slow, then plunge the metal sieve, compressing the grinds.

Poring myself a cup, seeking milk in the fridge, finding only Zoë's homemade almond milk. It will do. The almond milk adds a nutty flavor, keeps the bitterness of the coffee. A little more maple syrup combats this. The first fresh cup, I walk to the back porch.

I'm alone. Zoë's roommates are in Hawaii, they've been there for 4 weeks now, leaving just as I had returned. They'll be gone for another 3 months. They're trimming weed. Being alone feels nice.

The view is grandiose. In the distance the spires of Seattle rise, bursting beside a glistening Lake Washington, nested by vibrant green around the city. The morning is chilling; the coffee is warming. When rain begins I head inside. Zoë is downstairs now, preparing a simple breakfast of oatmeal.

"I like it here," I say.

"It's nice," She says, "Lake Forrest has strict ordinances regarding cutting trees. It's hard to do unless the tree is really causing damage or dying."

"It shows." Out the window the rain has begun strong, drenching the evergreen spread. "This is a nice house, too" I say.

"The owner's an architect. He built it for summer vacation or something." She says.

"I like it here," I repeat.

"That's good. The insulation is terrible, so it gets cold at times." She says.

"Still, it's nice."

Zoë smiles, turns the range down, "You could move in, for a few months at least while my roommates are away," she offers, pulling the oatmeal off the burner, chopping walnuts.

Her offer is simple and informal. She misses no step as the knife swiftly chops the walnuts, and moves on to apples, creating small piles of each, pushing them into single bowl when she needs more space. I watch for a second longer before turning away and walking to the kitchen nook with a bay window.

The offer repeats itself in my mind. In them are fear and excitement, confusion. Pulling the thread of each emotion, finding the source, is impossible. It's possible, this little domestic scene. I'm never sure of what it means, what I feel.

Bowls of oatmeal, fresh chopped nuts and fruit ready, Zoë brings two bowls to the nook, sets them on the table. She stands beside me, long fingers grasping my wrist, her other hand petting the nape of my neck.

It's soothing and tender and foreign. Everything — her, domesticity, comfort. I try and acclimate now, relax, thinking to myself: it could take a lifetime. This here is my lifetime. People wait lifetimes for this, something soothing, something tender. Chase it.

"Ok," I mumble, inaudible.

"Hmm?" Zoë asks.

"I'll move in, for a little bit anyway, I mean I can continue my sublet, he wants to anyway since his contract was renewed another 6 months, and ..." I stop, "I like it here."

"That's nice," Zoë says.

SEQUENCING MATTERS

The phone's ringing wakes me. Stumbling in the dark, tripping — Zoë's room still foreign — and finally finding the phone. A female voice begins to chirp at me, her first sentence lost in the groggy morning fog. Settling into awareness, I divine that the chirping alarm clock is Anne's assistant. She has questions, a list of them. Also there is press releases to approve. Can I come in she asks, Yes, Anne's Assistant I can come in.

"When?" She asks.

Whenever. Later. Later this afternoon or later another day. Another day, Anne's assistant, a never day... never ever never land.

But instead I say: "Today is fine."

Crawling back into bed, Zoë mumbles a question, who was that? My future, I say, collecting her in my arms. My future here, her. Your future is somewhere else. Why couldn't it include you? It doesn't. Zoë is here, and there is love. Damn it, there is love here.

The Gallery is empty when I arrive. From the back loft a chipper chirpy voice calls out, "Just a minute."

Waiting, examining the open space, the concrete floors, bright white walls, track lighting hanging from large steel beam rafters — a modern and clean space. Only a few pieces of art are hanging, oil acrylic pieces, all of them daunting in their super human size. The pieces have the sensibility of graffiti, vibrant colors, hard lines, all depicting a melancholy and manic rebellious ecstasy. They are impressive paintings. Reading the artist information plate I learn that the artist, and most of the work originates from Iran.

Her name is Abra. Forced from home due to the specter of political treason charges. People fear powerful art — it erodes control, challenges fear.

Brings me back, places where most don't go, hellholes others call home; where whispers of artists and agitators and journalist being taken in the night are common. Safety never guaranteed. Asking how many friends you have left is normal. I'm still here, on the other side, selling it all. Money's so damn silly. Chasing it, spending our time on it, and it almost makes no difference; life can snatch you in an instant, death or police or just random chaos. I expected you beside me my whole life. Expectations be damned. Are you ok out there? I'll pray for you. I can't pray. It's not real, too childish, too angry, and too hopeful.

An urge to walkout of the gallery fills me. Out the door, down the street to South Jackson, board the light rail, go right to SeaTac, not stopping. Maybe I'll find you out there. Find me.

And Zoë? I'm broken. She needs something whole. She told me no one is whole, we are all broken pieces, fragments made into mosaics and masterpieces.

132

"The proofs look fantastic." Anne's honey voice says from behind me.

Turning to face her, "Thank you," I say.

She stands beside me, examines the art-piece I was engaged with. "That's a fascinating piece, Abra smuggled it out of Iran, most of this stuff was, and she lost a lot of it; but this one made it." She stops, looks it over, "It's remarkable for how big it is to have managed to get it out."

"How'd she do it?" I ask.

"In Persian carpets, through a friend of hers that ran an export business." She answers. We admire the art for a moment longer.

"Where is everything going?" I ask, to change the subject.

Anne smiles, in her element, "Follow me."

"The opening sequence will be the young soldier in repose," she begins, leading me to a set of temporary white walls, "I love how peaceful it seems, they are playing cards, smoking, half-bored and yet alert... all of them just teenagers, and these guns right next to them. It humanizes war, forces us to see soldiers like our neighbors." She says. "Next," She turns a corner, "We'll hang the photos you have of the soldiers after battle, the guns in hand still..."

I hear Anne, but the words are far. Each photo group she lists returning to me.

"I think putting the two sets next to each other shows how fragile our humanity is, how easy it is to become killers..." She drones on.

Fuck, Anne, what do you know?

"I was thinking next we could set up the groups of photos you have of the blown apart city streets. We could really capture the visceral changes, the humans involved in war." Anne says. "Those grisly images you have.." (She shoots me a look that tells me I'm brave. No, Anne, I'm not brave, I'm insulated, desensitized) … "there's child with the lost eye, the old man with the missing fingers …"

Lost, lost, lost, all the world lost in the fire and brimstone of war; neatly captured to evoke visceral evocative feelings in your comfortable activist viewer.

Damn it Anne, your viewers are going to walk in here feeling clean, and their going to leave that way. What they see here is momentary, a single stop on the evening carousel; part of the cultural experience. Dinner, Art, Wine. Maybe the college kids come — part of an assignment. Most breezing through, a single stop before hunting down drugs and booze, fumbling with each other in the dark.

There might be one, touched in some part of their brain; signals firing off as they think: I found what I'm going to do. Call me — after you lose your first friend, watch a stranger bleed, slow and painfully, into oblivion … I'll tell you: That's life. I'm not trying to sound like Clint Eastwood, a caricature. But, that is life. Messy and short.

Then the last series, Anne stops speaking, just shows me the proofs. Even the most slick words fail here, looking at children trapped in conflict. It was a devastating collection to create. I remember asking this dead-eyed girl, maybe she was 7, to stand still holding her toy. Asking her to stand still was a formality. She wasn't moving, wasn't bounding about with energy and preciousness. Just a shell-shocked veteran. With kids you see the word shell-shocked. They haven't developed masks yet, the ability to keep pain in, to hide it, to drink or smoke till its gone. They're empty: shells. Disgusted and amazed at the cruelty of the world: shocked. Shell-shocked. Every single child.

We age and trade youth for wisdom. They age and trade youth for violence.

Every damn photo I see you there.

Why?

I don't know. You didn't grow up with war and violence, you're not there.

But.

I keep looking for you in those children, hoping to find you.

And I think of you and Anne drones on. Droll, slick Anne coming to her crescendo.

Great, wonderful, magnifique!

Whatever days and times you want, Je sui très accommodating.

An interview? I must? Fine, fine, just get me out of here.

Outside. The crispness of spring makes you feel alive. I vomit. Stumble to a cafe. Call Zoë.

"Pick me up, please?" I implore.

THE THINGS WE DO FOR A CUNT.

For 3 weeks I ignore the interviewer's calls. Zoë intervenes on his behalf. She picked up his call, arranges a meeting.

"It'll be good, an opportunity." She describes it.

Embrace change, she implores.

I call the interviewer, day of, to confirm. His name is Nathan. Recent graduate from some rarefied exclusive eastern institution. Cheerful man-boy.

"Dr Livingstone, I presume," He answers his cell.

"Cute." I say.

He's still smiling, "You're a bit of a recluse, and usually people wait till they're famous for that."

"You want your interview?" I say.

"No, but Seattle City Arts does, and I want to pay rent." He says.

I laugh, "Ok, then, let's finish it off." I say.

"How's Elliot Bay Cafe sound, around 4?"

"See you then."

I arrive late. Nathan is already there, a gentle face man, thin, bearded, neatly coiffed hair. Nerd-chic. He's waiting at a two-top table, I can tell it's him by the equipment: digital recorder, small notepad. He's reading a selection of Hemingway shorts, "The Short Happy Life of Francis Macomber."

"You like it?" I ask, seating myself.

Nathan slowly places the book down, smiles brightly. "I enjoy Hemingway. You ever read his works?"

"I've a friend who loves him. Not much though, I only read in the field and then you just read what's around. I've read 'For Whom the Bell Tolls", an ex got it for me."

"What did you think of it?"

"I see why she got for me." I say.

Nathan nods, trying to decipher my answer, trying to find the best volley. "Did it mean anything to you?"

"The book or why she got it?"

"Either."

"I don't dissect literature."

"Sure, but you gotta have a response to it..."

"Nothing worth your time."

"Ok."

"Let's do this as quick and painlessly as possible." I say.

"Shouldn't be a problem, it's just an art mag." Nathan shrugs.

"Lovely, so what's the question." I snap.

"Tell me about the project, is it something you had in mind all these years?" he asks, still smiling.

"No."

"So then why take all those photos? What motivated you?"

"It was what I was paid for."

"All right, why choose to get paid for something like that?"

"Why'd you choose your work?"

"I like it most of the time, this isn't ideal, you're not the Obama's but it's a start."

"There you go." I sneer.

"You like what you do? Despite how difficult it is?"

"Enough, I suppose."

"Is enough enough?"

'What are you asking?" I say.

He pauses, regroups, "How do you keep your sense of self and humor intact in difficult places like that?"

"I thought this was just an art mag?"

Nathan shrugs, "You take difficult pictures and make evocative portraits of it, it must affect you, your out look."

I look back, thinking, recalling: I remember in Lebanon once, when I was just starting, a warm night, a small cafe, I was drinking coffee and anise liquor. The proprietor and I got along well. I enjoyed listening to him. An explosion happened, maybe 3 blocks away; close enough to hear it − get the cortisol rising, the heart pumping wildly, hear the shouts of people. The shop owner remaining unfazed, pours me whiskey walks it over. Tells me to relax. Relax? Relax, he insists. With death and dying everywhere around me? He pours me a little more. Death and dying are everywhere anyway, here it just shouts a little louder. So what do you do? Relax and laugh a little louder. How the fuck does that work? He pats my back, laughs, you laugh he says. Laughter defy's death he tells me.

I say to Nathan, "You adjust."

"Do you have an intent with each shot? A goal in mind?"

Intent? None of it is intentional. You don't intend to stumble into war and walk away with images of destruction. Every success on my end was one more tally against humanity.

"No, Nathan, you're not allowed intent." I say.

"What do you mean?"

"Everything happens at once, and then you act."

"Do you ever have to put yourself in danger to get a shot you want?"

"Yes, every fucking shot, every fucking time is dangerous, and you don't get time to think of angles or placement or what you want. You act and you don't die. That's all it is. It's an instinct and you suck at first, but you're lucky, and later you stay lucky but get better. You try and start to think, really think, you invite trouble."

I can see Nathan trying to understand. Just like Anne he doesn't. Like everyone who is going to peruse that gallery.

I don't want to explain it: how when the adrenaline floods your brain and the whole world starts to come awake, and the latent instincts that keep you alive bubble to the surface, and everything around you slows to crawl, even though you know it's happening at the speed of life. You think to yourself : this is Einstein's god, relativity. You know death is right beside you, you even see people hurt and dying right next to you… and you've never been more alive. Nothing trivial or significant passes in your thoughts, just moments. This, then; the next. I don't want to explain that to you because you'll never understand it. Just take your notes, jot down my pain, display it for the gallery goers and let them have their fantasies, just don't ask me to explain it.

"What do you hope to achieve?" Nathan asks.

How do I answer? Well, my friend wanted a nice cunt. He sold my photographs for it. "There's no achievement, it's a proof… like math." I say.

"Proof of what?" Nathan asks.

"That God doesn't exist." I say, snort.

God is perfect, that's the idea. But nothing is perfect. You were, still are. Zoë maybe. Perfect by virtue of being enough.

"I've had enough." I say, interrupting Nathan's latest question.

Nathan has more questions still though.

"Tell them I tried, but I'm a damaged recluse. Make it sound however the fuck you want. I'm done."

I excuse myself. Nathan remains sitting, face looks flummoxed. He starts to argue, smooth talk to get me to sit again, anything... Sorry, Nathan, I'm not listening. It's not your fault, don't blame yourself.

GOOD THINGS COME TO PEOPLE.

Outside is grey, night is arriving. I feel spry and chipper. I call Icon, hoping he's in Seattle.

"YO!!! Big J." He picks up.

"I-connie, what you doing?"

"Drinking coffee, feeling good."

"Where at?"

"Cafe Vita, dude, in Seattle."

"Which one?"

"On the hill."

That's just around the corner. "Want to meet?" I ask.

"Hum, what you thinking? I'm just finishing up a meeting here."

"Let's get weird." I say.

"YeaH! Let's do it. I gotta go, she's coming back from the bathroom. Just come over here." He says.

I hang up. Start to feel lightness, elation.

Turning the corner, thinking about Nathan, about Anne, about CityArts, and the whole circus. Fuck it. Fuck them. Fuck the show. Fuck war.

Coming upon the cafe, Icon is sitting with a stranger to me. She has a luminous face, an active intelligence to her manner. She's swank and distinctive. For a moment I watch them: Icon's explosive conversational hands, and exuberance; her calculating and charming face that hides its motivations well. The scene is so perfect, bright. I'm tempted to leave it be, keep walking. Leave them in that momentary peace. That's what you wanted for me right, peace? Instead I want a hard drink, the warmth spreading in me, no more fear when I feel, no more Anne and Nathan and the database of past imagines.

Before I walk off, Icon spies me. He smiles, waves, opens his arms to the sky, gestures to me to enter.

I smile back, enter. Inside the whirring of the espresso grinder, the smell of roasted coffee beans, the trendy rustic cafe bursting with ticking energy. Order a coffee, sit down, the stranger is strange no more: Lydia.

She extends a hand with a slight tilt of her head that asks who I am, what use I might have.

"Lydia is a promoter," Icon explains.

She nods, swishes a tooth-pick from one corner of her mouth to the next, tells me of an upcoming show. There is an ardor to her depiction of the event. I enjoy it, though I don't follow. It's nice to care about the irreverent I think; those things that don't matter, and yet do.

As Lydia's excitement grows I notice how the corner of her eyes tighten, as if they were attempting to smile. You did that. Remember? It was Autumn, in Rhode Island when I first noticed it. We were sailing and you didn't believe I could steer. I did, though badly. Later when you were recounting my failure I saw that expressive crinkle for the first time.

From then on, I always noticed. It came fleetingly, when you told a story you were enamored with: like the time in Mexico, when the turtle came to shore to lay eggs and we sat together and watched the ritual. The turtle was crying. You wanted to believe it was because it would leave its young and she was so sad because she couldn't stay. I told you, no, it's just a part of the physiology, the secretion of extra salt. That amazed you. For months you read about the sea-turtle, their habits and habitats and numbers and threats. You were heart-broken when you learned how long-line fisheries would pull them on the hook for miles and hours in what was a slow torturous death drag.

I couldn't feel what you felt. I didn't understand how life could be so cruel, how it threatens us.

Now I know. Life is nothing but cruel, it gives to take. It's the secret of life, that it will consume everything.

These thoughts, I don't share. Instead, just smile for the stranger and never let on about what bustles beneath. People are delicate. Let them learn the cost of life at their own speed.

Icon smiles at me, touches my shoulder. "How is it?"

"I just had an interview with City Arts," I say.

"Really? That's awesome." Icon is beaming, "Are you excited?"

I shrug.

"Dude, that is awesome. It's great." Icon says, turning to Lydia, "his photos are gonna be showing at a gallery... which one, again, I forgot?" he asks me.

"Whitesmith Gallery," I say.

"That's a nice one," Lydia comments, "What kind of photos are they," she asks.

"Conflict photography." I answer

"Oh," She thinks, "Were you ever in combat?"

"No." I say.

Icon steps in, "They're really good, some of them are tough, but it's all really good. When's the show?"

"Three weeks from now is the opening. They'll be hanging for 6 weeks after that."

Lydia nods, "I'll check it out. Any one need another coffee?"

"Coffee sounds nice, thanks," I say.

Icon looks over me, sincere faced, asks me, "Are you ok?"

Brush him off, yes fine, "Let's get weird tonight," I say.

"Yeah?" Icon lights up, "You want to get weird? Yeah? Let's do it." He smiles, claps, "Getting' weird." His voice is sing song.

"Should we call Sean?" I ask.

"Yeah! I love that guy." Icon says.

Lydia returns, hands me a coffee.

"What has you two so excited?" She asks.

"Getting weird tonight!" Icon preaches.

Weird?" Lydia asks.

"Weird," I confirm.

"Hey-yo, what we getting weird on?" Icon asks.

"What we got?" I ask.

"Coffee. Apple Juice.!" Icon exclaims.

"Apple juice?" Lydia inquires.

"Whiskey." I clarify.

"Apple Juice." Icon says.

"I love me some apple juice." I say

"What else?" Icon asks, straightening his pointer, placing it on his temple, eyes looking upward, "How about listening to Motown."

I shrug, "Yeah, Motown."

"Downtown with Motown." Icon says, followed by a high pitched shriek like clattering-call.

Lydia nods, smiles, "You boys have fun."

"Join?" Icon asks.

She shakes her head, "No. Too much work and a show tonight."

"Right show," Icon says, "Maybe we'll go."

"I'll put you and a plus one on the guest list." She says.

"Thank you." I say.

She turns to me, sizing me, "Good luck with your show." Turning back to Icon, "Don't forget about following up on the things we talked about."

"Yeah, I got it." Icon says.

Lydia gathers herself, leaving. We say goodbye. Watch her leave. She walks with a determined grace.

"Yo, I'm going to teach a workshop and dance for some dope DJs, paid fest work."

"Congrats." I say.

"Yeah, good stuff, all around" Icon says, sits back.

"Hmph" I snort.

"Ah man, it's good. All of it. Responsibility, growing, learning... you doing the photo-thing, I'm doing the dance thing... it's good." He explains.

I nod, agree, "Sure, it's all wonderful." I say, "Let's get drunk."

Icon laughs, "Ok."

IT REALLY IS THAT FUCKING EASY.

Hours later, at Lo-Fi, in the back room, skunk-drunk. Only illicit powders, sassy, keeping me ambulatory. Sean is here, he met us earlier. We ate food somewhere, fish sandwiches. By then Icon and I were near-drunk, Zoë called around then, asking when I'd get home. At least, my phone says she called, and I assume she has those questions. I'll be home after I've been drunk.

Outside of Lo-Fi, a tender rain, partiers, dressed to kill, smoking, killing themselves. Following Sean, Icon, two girls in fishnets and ragged-fur, to one of the girl's car. They have cocaine, Columbian marching powder, yeah, ok, why not? Cocaine, sassafras, booze, a cycle as wonderful as the rain tapping us. All the substances keep you warm. Back inside: bass, rhythm, melody; outside: snort, swig, dip. This will all cost me, sure, I know, but the bill isn't due just yet, the night is young.

From Lo-Fi to Monkey Loft (ETG), a second story loft-club open till 4 a.m. Everyone with dilated pupils, false buzzing. They'll all pay that bill too. Same routine as Lo-fi — in, music; out, libations. Icon texts Zoë for me. She wishes me a good night with the boys.

Eventually even the after-hours closes. Sean, Icon, and I manage to slither to Sean's hi-rise condo. The fancy exterior facade giving way to fancy interiors, to fancy apartment — our very own den of iniquity. Sean produces a fine Japanese scotch, Nikka barrel-aged 15 years — in my honor he claims — for the coming debut. 2 weeks till.

Wave it off, "I'll drink your fancy scotch, but leave out the honor guard."

Icon looks ready to argue, then instead shakes his head and laughs as I snatch the bottle and drink.

"Apple juice?" I ask, proffering the bottle to Icon.

"I love apple juice." Icon says, taking the bottle. He swigs.

Sean seizes back his bottle, "We all do."

"You moving here permanently?" I ask Icon.

"I dunno, maybe? I like it." He answers.

"He's become a semi-permanent couch surfer," Sean asserts.

"Thank you, you're so kind," Icon grasps Sean's shoulder. Sean hands him the amber bottle with a smile, he drinks, passes it to me.

I hold it, gently, like a new-born child; swig slowly.

"And you?" Icon asks

"Me?" I say

"Yeah, you. You going find you own place or keep playing house?" Sean snarks.

I take a second, longer pull of whiskey, hold the bottle in front of me, "This is good."

Sean snatches it, "Fuck off, you want more, then come clean."

I pause, look lovingly at the bottle, "I dunno. It's not meant to be a long term solution."

"So you're looking for a place?"

"Sort of."

"Sort of?" Sean snorts, "Sort of … how long you been there?"

"2 months or so."

"Da-yum, 2 months." Icon whistles.

Sean laughs, "The temps at my office don't even last 2 months."

"So?" I say.

"So," Sean passes the bottle to Icon, who swallows a lot quickly, then hands the bottle to me, " a passive decision is still a decision."

"Yo, dude, are you happy?" Icon asks.

Happy? I drink. What is that? But I know — I was happy, once. You encouraged it. Smiled for me. That made me happy. It's silly how happy I was. Maybe it's all used up? Someone said: Happiness is available, take some. But what about what life takes? You found happiness in the most insignificant things: the way my teeth marked an apple, how a bug hopped, savage sunlight on a half empty glass of rose`...

Then I recall a moment: Zoë is happy, smiling. I asked her what she was happy about, waking next to you, she said. That's remarkable I think, that one of us can feel it.

Am I happy? Sometimes I am: when Zoë laughs at nothing, these heaping gulps of laughter as if she'd drown in it; or when she curls into me like a cat, reading or idling...

"I think so, I don't know." I tell Icon.

I drink more. Sean brings out Cocaine and Ketamine.

"Louis CK!" Icon says.

Sean smirks as he cuts the white powders together on a portable mirror, lining them up neatly, passing the mirror, "I don't know he says... You're not happy J, you never will be. You don't know how and that poor girl hasn't figured that out yet, and she loves you."

I wince, snort the powdered mix, drink again, "It's not so fucking easy, ok?"

Sean is watching me, Icon is silent, looks tense. Then Sean smiles, "Of course it isn't." He sounds empathetic. Like that it deflates.

"Anyways, It's nice now and sometimes I love her and ... sometimes I am happy." I say.

Icon reaches out to me, his hand envelopes my shoulder, "You'll learn, man. You'll be ok."

I nod. I'll learn. I smile. I can be happy. It's hard, that's all. Being happy is so damn hard.

Outside the light of dawn spreads, the world opening to the subtle grey and orange light. Sure, I'll learn to be happy, it's just that fucking easy.

WE ALL HAVE ROUTINES

I remember a clear cold morning, stunted oak, sporadic pines, and sage brush spread out over the rolling horizon, hiding the border of Israel and Lebanon. Two Israeli soldiers walk with me, Tal and Ofir. Both are young, serious men. Tal long and sinewy with a broad face; Ofir stout, strong, a careful man with a tight mischievous smile. Both comfortable in uniforms, IMI Galil assault rifles dangling like well worn purses from their shoulders.

Tal was talking about old black and white movies, asking questions about framing and composition. I answered what I could. Ofir only half-listened. Both Tal and Ofir maintained a subtle alertness. We were on routine patrol. The night before we had gotten drunk on an anise liquor, drinking a thick clove coffee in the morning to wash out the hangover.

Once Tal exhausted his knowledge of film, we walked in silence. Periodically Ofir would offer short anecdotes and history lessons. Tal would occasionally and exuberantly interrupt to color the politics. It was all very personal.

I listened carefully, trying to understand. It was futile. I didn't live it. They tried to convey it to me still, the way a gentle teacher might try and explain, for the 12th time, calculus to a failing Algebra student. The day continued. Occasionally we'd see the sporadic construction of homes that symbolized the conflict.

The heat became taxing soon enough. We stopped at a rocky overhang, a canteen of water coming around.

"She is very sweet in the desert, yes?" Ofir said.

"What?" I asked

"Maim ... eh, you know, wah-ter." He said. "Always, eh, you learn to love what you don't have."

I nodded in agreement, saying nothing. I continued to look outward, wondering about lack, and conflict and humans and why. Beside me Ofir and Tal chatted idly in Hebrew.

Then it happened.

Just like that.

Like life happens.

Suddenly, like how you left.

I felt light, my mouth going dry, no panic… Ofir and Tal spoke — nothing I could decipher. Heat came first, blistering heat. Next the rising smoke, dust, burning sulfur and gun powder smell. I recall running, hiding behind boulders, waiting, running, keeping close to Ofir and Tal. One of them was speaking rapidly into a radio device. The words sounded jumbled, my hearing temporarily lost.

We stopped running. I don't know how much we ran. Ofir checks us for injuries. I was ok. We all were.

We waited. Nothing.

It was over.

Like that.

Suddenly.

Like you.

It was my first experience with a rocket missile.

What stands out now is how routine it was. A routine patrol, a routine attack. So very much like god-damned life.

MISSILES ALL EXPLODE

We have routine — Zoë and I.

It works.

Then suddenly …

"I want to talk." She says.

"Ok."

"Not now, but soon." She says.

"Are you ok?" I ask, each word thick.

"I don't know." She says. Lips pursed. Words hollow.

"Can we talk now?" I ask, frightened.

She pauses, "No. Right now, let's enjoy your opening. It's your first." She smiles politely.

I don't push. We leave together to the Gallery.

AN EXPLOSION LIKE A WHIMPER

Forty five minutes before the public opening, Zoë and I are drinking wine in the Gallery's upper-loft. Annie is humming beside us, fussing over the last particular details with the lighting technician, the caterer, the media consultant, and her phone.

Between each snapped order she assures me: "It's expected to be a wonderful turn out. That little stunt of yours during the interview turned out to be rather more helpful than I expected." She smiles, smug smile, "He even gave us positive reviews."

Us? I think, Us? Sure why not, us. War is just art, been that way for at least 2,500 years ... war is deception, too ... and what's a little deception between friends, right, Anne? We got a wonderful review!

Anne commandeers Zoë, explaining the genius of the layout to her, praising my photos. Zoë remains stoic.

Zoë, what are you thinking?

I can't watch them anymore, I wander off. Zoë follows, leaving Anne gape mouthed, mid-sentence. I turn, try to face

Zoë. She shifts, slightly, facing the hung photos. She's looking at a picture of a ruined market-center, an old man amidst the rubble, standing beside his rag-tag cart, still trying to sell the last few grains he has to sell, everything in ruins. I hear a small sound, I think Zoë is mumbling my name. I start towards her. I stop. My hand goes out, rests on her shoulder. She's crying. Pulling closer, she's asking me in a whisper: "What's wrong with you? Why is this so hard for you?"

I don't know. Don't have answers.

Weakly we walk back to the upper loft, step onto the rooftop deck, the fading autumn brings a cold night, bright moon.

"Almost a year," I say.

"8 months," she corrects me.

I still can't answer what's wrong.

A city alley sits below us, stench of piss and stale beer rising to us.

"I'm here," She says, measured tone, words heavy, "But I won't stay here if you're not here."

She turns and heads back inside. I can only think: she's right.

Looking up absently, clouds move in and out of view quickly, stars disappearing, appearing. Still feeling alone. Confused. About love, about giving, about receiving.

Not loss. I know losing.

It's never easy, the first time or the last. At last you lose yourself. Until then: get up, keep going, I can't go on, I will go on. There's no choice in the matter. None of it fucking matters. Oh, but, it does.

It does and I want only to escape, except there are no easy exits and the only way out is in, right into the middle of the fray.

I can see the crowd now inside. It is a wonderful turn-out Anne, it really is. So many pretty, fine dressed people. Connoisseur's of culture — life's ultimate distraction.

Well, then, into the fray, as I enter the Gallery and descend the steps from the loft into the main space.

Inside: the chill of the city replaced by the comfort of radiant heating. For a few moments I can bask in anonymity. It dissipates with the appearance of Anne. She descends, that shark smile, a flash flood of words, feet steeping to a quick tango I can't hear as she leads me: here, there, everywhere is someone to know, to be introduced to, work with, work for, be inspired by… she presents each person like a business card. Business cards of cashmere and wine and fine lace and atypical style. Business cards that compliment me, analyze my psyche in veiled questions and comments built for reaction. Sympathizing and understanding in vague slow nods and platitudes, blending together into a single blur, voices becoming indistinguishable babble. And all the tension that began my evening becomes panic.

Slipping away from Anne, ducking behind a wall, trying to hold on — everything is so strange: these privileged men and women milling about and looking at stills of destruction, loss and pain.

What color…

How arresting...

How sad...

When is the sitter leaving again...

How intense...

What are we supposed to write about...

Is it really so bad...

I love there atmosphere...

What can we do...

I need a drink...

It's almost beautiful ...

Dizziness, the desire to vomit. Closing my eyes. I want to understand. I want sanity. I want to find Zoë.

A hand gently rest itself on my shoulder.

It's a woman. Zoë? Elation.

I turn.

No.

It's Laurie.

"Been a while stranger." She smiles.

I only nod.

"This is your show, right?" She asks, smiling still.

"It is." I mumble, glancing around the room in broad sweeps.

"I recognized you in City Arts." She says.

"Thanks," I say, looking for an opening, trying to slide away.

Laurie grabs me by the bicep, softly, and still iron-clad.

"Who are you looking for?" She asks.

"Zoë... partner..." I mumble, still scanning for her.

Laurie nods, "She's fine, I'm sure. Relax. Enjoy this." She encompasses the room in her gaze, "This is a rare thing."

I listen, take a few deep breaths, "I'm still not sue it's what I want." I say.

"You have it, though." She counters.

I shrug. "Still."

"I think it's wonderful." She says.

I crack a small smile. "So do I, I guess." With that I slip into a roving gaggle of college kids, continue a furious scan of the crowd.

She's nowhere. I wonder if she's left. The thought devastates me. And yet ... it'd be easier. How easy would it be ... returning to that emptiness, like after you.

Only, she is here.

I find her in the corner of a room, looking outward at the whole show.

"I though you left," I approach delicately.

She smiles, "No." It's the most tender no I have ever heard.

"Would you like to?" I ask.

"If you want." She says.

"Please." I reach out my hand. She takes it.

As we are leaving, she asks me, "What about all your friends that came?"

"It doesn't matter." I say, her hand in mine, stepping into the crisp air, biting. It feels electric. I start to run, she runs with me. We keep running, aimlessly. Two blocks away we stop, breathless. Look up, look around, looking wildly. Everything is bright, shimmering. I laugh. Zoë laughs. Together our laughter grows, ringing like bells, lifting us. For a moment laughter cures everything.

Feeling light and hollow, I grip Zoë. She smiles, shakes free, kisses me, and begins to walk. I follow, quiet, by her side.

We reach the Sound, the lightness of laughter has left us, it feels heavy again. The water looks purple. The light of the port and ferris wheel glitter. Boats pass. Conversations from walkers come to us in snatches:

"I heard she …"

"Hell, No, I won't…"

"Reach out to him …"

"…She left anyway."

"… It's not easy, ok?"

"…Who wants ice cream?…"

"Give me a cigarette."

"…It's too hard anyway…"

Each snippet floats on, carrying itself into the ether, dying out as life dictates.

I look at Zoë, try to decipher her intent stare into the sound, note the chill breeze reddening her cheeks, the way her nostrils flare out with every breath, the tight way she holds he mouth… there is so much to say.

Instead I turn towards the water, staring with her. It's easy to just stare out into that space, to wonder about whats out there, about you, where you've gone.

"I found the letters you've been writing." Her voice is soft and steady.

No words form to answer. The small joy I felt, the quiet paean, hardens and dies. We stand for minutes in silence, a cold wind lifts from the sound. Zoë shivers.

"Are you cold?" I ask.

"No." She says.

"Ok." I have nothing left to say.

Silence continues.

"What's going on?" I'll listen." She says. Each word is calibrated and weighted.

Nod. That's all I can do. A few words attempt to start, but end inside me.

"It's cold. Can we walk?" I ask, finally, to answer her stone stare.

"Fine." She says.

Movement begins, it feels kind. Urges to run, never stop, begin. Ignoring them, reaching outward for Zoë's hand. She refuses.

"I need clarity. I'm not sure what's going on, but I need clarity." She states.

"You do." I say.

"So, what's going on?" She demands.

Shake my head. It'd be so easy to talk. No it won't. It's hard. Talking now means facing you. I don't want to face you. I can't face you. It'd be good, nice even. No. I can't. I will. I won't.

"Just … I … it's nothing … I … fuck." I shrug. That's all I can give her. Everything, she wants to give me everything and I all can give her is a pocket full of mumbles and a shrug.

It's enough for her to know: It's not enough.

Both of us know. And all the laughter, the little smiles, the shared bed, all of them know too: it's not enough.

Tell her, I think.

Sometimes I want to.

But I won't.

We walk back to her car, hollow silence, each step a condemnation. The car spurs to life. Silence. Driving home. Silence. At home, her home, the home I'm trying to make my own, she looks at me... and I can't decipher: is it pity? Disgust? Confusion? Hurt? I don't know.

"Good night." She says, leaving me alone in the kitchen, the lights off, just the sliver of illumination from the moon left.

SOME LISTS YOU DON'T CHECK TWICE.

An hour is gone, and rain has begun. It's soft against the window, and watching it feels nice. I step outside, walk to the back of the house, the ground is buoyant and tender. Each foot fall is noiseless. I stop at the ax, consider chopping wood, don't.

Back inside with warm earl-grey tea. The rain is constant. I watch it. The tea is at the dregs, but I still bring the cup to my lips, still hoping maybe something remains.

That's how it's always been since you.

But.

But what?

Nothing. Nothing changes except for all of it.

All I can do is face it.

Getting up, walking to the kettle, nothing remains, setting the cup beside it. Kettle and mug, the perfect pair, so damn smug, flaunting their purpose.

Get a grip, I think. Breath coming truncated and broken. I feel broken. Reset, I think. Back to default— run, run like hell.

But you told me once: you can't run from the pain, go towards it.

Like hell I will. I'm running. Watch me run — out run everything.

Quietly upstairs, into our shared room. Pack, that's all I think.

What do I need?Not much.

Systematically proceed through the check-list, a checklist I've done hundreds of times.

Clothing. Check. Just enough, is all.

Pause, look over to the bed. She's barely stirred, asleep. So fucking peaceful. Frighteningly so. So beautiful. But I can't stay. I'll take all her peace. It's better for her if I go. I know how. Practiced.

Everything I need is collected, the remainder: my equipment, my letters, the rest of my life, is downstairs. I think to kiss Zoë goodbye, even hovering beside the bed, leaning over, hovering above her. It's daunting how beautiful she is. Observing: that French nose, slight olive skin, her almond eyes, closed, eyes that light up with curiosity and desire. I want that. Let her keep it.

I don't kiss her. I can't. I'm a coward, I know it.

Grabbing my meager belongings, shoving them into my pack, slowly walking out.

Gently, with as little noise as possible, I close the door.

Gut-wrenching pain hits me. I'm crying, sobbing without sound. Composing myself, turning away, walking down the stairs. Everything is lucid — alive, like the moments before crossing the amorphous space that marks the fragile border between the peace and conflict.

Once across you never come return exactly the same, even in the times where nothing happens, no consequences; you come back a little emptier, as if you live the consequences of others. Everyone suffers consequences.

Downstairs, I quietly text for a cab. I instruct that they pick me up at the driveways end. A text flash informs me I have 35 minutes. Enough time to gather the last of my things.

The camera bag is ready. Old habits and not dying, or some such. All I have left is some books, a computer ... Many things will be left behind:

> -4 coffee mugs
> (Recently bought in London, beautiful ceramic pieces. They were elegant, and reminded me of something Zoë had once liked)
> -A high end burr coffee grinder
> (I do bring a small portable grinder in my bag. Coffee is gold in the field.)
> -7 rolls of undeveloped film
> (Photos of Zoë: camping, eating a cake, drinking tea with knees curled into her, reading ... other images of things I don't recall.)
> -A small collection of records:
> > Hot Chip

Hot Chip
Jessie Ware
Devotion
Rolling Stones
Exile On Main Street
Miles Davis
Kind of Blue
Blockhead
Music By Cavelight
-A pair of snow shoes
(Used only 6 times, twice with Zoë)
-A collection of water colors
(Zoë had gifted them to me, sometime
after I told her how my childhood was
dominated by thick paper and changing
colors...I had used the set only once.)

As I catalogue what remains a text arrives: Cab is here. Packing the trunk, all I am taking neatly bagged up... my life, compact and moveable.

The driver asks: "Where to?"

I blink, look at him, he's tall, has the style of an old school Rockabilly. He asks again, and I give him an address. He grunts, slams the trunk, slides into the driver seat. A minute passes before I move. I get in the cab, linger before closing the door. The taxi wheels spin, crunching gravel, rolling on, moving, going.

Not looking back, but thinking: Zoë ...
I left Zoë.

Add that to the list.

-Zoë
(The first woman I loved since you. Zoë,
composed of her odd affectations, of the

unflinching will to be kind and forgive, the
lopsided smile that betrayed the childish
notions brewing in her mind, the shake of
a thigh, like ripples to my spine, the
pecking kiss of her thin lips, the smell of
her)

And that's it, I think: it's an ending. Not a fairy tale,
because there is no such thing as fairy tales.

On the radio plays a song that sounds like 80's soft jazz
with modern disco drums moving us along south into
downtown. All I can hear are the lyrics, a chastising refrain:
"fall asleep right next me, you know you were never good
enough..." with the last three words of the chorus just sung
so sweet and devastating.

The driver comes to a stop, "23.76, please" He says.

Breaking my trance, handing him cash, stepping outside,
I'm on 12th and Pike. It's 3 a.m., the streets are quiet except
for a few drunks, some drifters. It's barren. I'm alone.
Everything I have, everything, here with me. I want to shout.
Staying silent, walking to a building, looking up Shawn's
name on the intercom. Punching the code in, the phone
ringing... a weary voice answers.

BREAKFAST IS FOR CHAMPIONS AND CHUMPS ALIKE

The next morning, slate grey sky, no rain. Looking out to the city below from 12 stories up. Coffee grinding itself in the background. An escalating piano sound begins to play, shuffling begins from Shawn's room.

When the grinder finishes I bring out a French press. 4 scoops of grinds, cinnamon, touch of sugar; and returning to the loft window. Looking down makes me dizzy, sick almost. Soon I hear Shawn in the kitchen, pouring himself coffee. He takes a sip, walks to the fridge, pours milk into the cup, "So, what the fuck?" He says.

I shrug.

"That's it? That's all you have to say for yourself? A shrug? You wake me at 3 in the morning, looking like you're moving in, and all you can do is shrug?" Shawn says.

Turning to him, he doesn't look angry. He's calm. It disappoints me. Maybe I wanted to see him angry... see an explosion, something visceral... some emotion I am devoid of.

In the kitchen I pour myself coffee, "Yea, it's all I got," I say.

Sean stares, shakes his head. Traffic is increasing below us, people rushing to work, blaring horns, the city goes on. "I don't know. I can't explain it." I say.

"That's evident." Shawn says, "You're really fucking up man, you keep hiding from everything, not facing things, afraid, and the end result is you fuck my up my night and fuck up my morning, and probably fuck up your damn life, too. Which is fine, but you're dragging me down, and her down, and everyone else who gives a shit."

"I know." I say.

"I know, he says, Jesus."

"What more do you want?"

"Me? Nothing. It's not what I want, it's you and that pack over there and the running and the inability to be a fucking adult and know that shit is sad sometimes and things hurt and things are good too…So it's not me, it's you." Sean says.

"Then why give me shit? Why give a fuck at all?" I ask.

"Cause you're fucking up my breakfast, asshole. It's the most important meal of the day and your making it all sad and shitty." He says.

"Cornflakes goes great with sad and shitty." I say.

Sean chuckles, "Yeah, but I'm serious. Stop fucking things up."

"Next time." I say.

"Did you love her? It sure as hell looked like you did." He asks.

"I don't…"

"What? You don't know? You know. You're not that fucking dumb. You know, and you probably did, but all you know how to be is a mopey narcissistic asshole."

"Fuck off, you're the narcissist." I say.

"I'm not the one with the suitcase leaving the first positive thing in my life."

"I don't need your judgement."

"Yeah you do. Cause you're fucking up and we don't live forever and even if your not a narcissist, you're definitely a masochist… this is easily one of the shittiest decision I'm watching you make in real time. You can make it, but you're fucking up snd you're going to regret this one real fast. I know you."

"I hear you. I get it." I say.

"No you don't." He says. "But it doesn't matter. I'm going to go to work, you're going to fuck things up. My spare key is here," He points to a drawer, "The door code is 3667. You have a week here. One week then I want you out of here."

"Ok." I say. He leaves, I walk to the drawer and find the spare key. Palming it, closing my hand into a fist, feeling it's sharpness dig into my skin.

ADDICTIONS ARE HABITS YOU CAN'T KLL.

Time loses coherence.

With nothing to engage me, no routine, no schedules for time to adhere to, time acts oddly.

The week Sean gave me slinks off, drunkenly, angrily, returning to me with a thud. All I could claim for the week was languid sips of whiskey, coffee, aimless walks at all hours, and the old fears coming back, burying their seeds me.

On the last day of the ultimatum I make a choice.

I dial a number, "Tina." I say.

"It's been awhile," She says.

"Got anywhere I can go?"

"There always is, always. But I don't want to send you anywhere." She says.

"Why not?"

"I'm getting soft, I like you, I guess." She says.

"Great, so do me this favor."

"God-damn Jaleel, I was hoping to never hear from you again."

"Too late for that."

There is a long pause on the other end, punctured by the metallic snap of an old zippo lighter, the faint flick of flint.

"Why the fuck are you calling me Jaleel." Tina asks.

"Work."

"Bullshit. You don't need work. I've seen what you're doing now, the write-ups, the gallery, hear you're getting fashion work... you don't need this shit."

"I want to do it. It's... it's like home."

A sharp inhalation occurs, Tina coughs. " You know my doc told me my lungs are like 63. I'm 47. My lungs are 16 years older than me, they can have a sweet 16, for christsakes. And, you know, I'm still fucking smoking."

"You still roll your own?"

"Yeah, but I compromised, I only smoke at night now." Tina says. "Only, the problem is most of my waking hours happen when it's dark out, so my compromise isn't much of a compromise... Basically it doesn't mean shit."

"I'll take whatever you got, AP wire, long form, whatever." I say, "Just get me a ticket somewhere."

"Can't fucking stop... that's all. Just gonna keep smoking..." She says, "Ok, I have a kid who was doing some images for a long piece slated for Atlantic... in Israel, he booked it back home cause one of his family members got cancer... sad shit, really. You know the Gaza area, its just documenting more of the same shit, really. They've been at for 5,000 years or so now."

"Great. How soon can I fly out?"

"I'll talk to Pete over at the Atlantic in the a.m., and if that's in order I'd say 4-5 days assuming your passport is up to date."

"It is."

"Ok, I'll call you tomorrow, maybe you'll have come to your senses then."

She hangs up. The dial tone is soothing.

STUPID IS AS STUPID.

The next morning, Seattle still grey, in Sean's kitchen, "Six days?" Sean asks.

"Yeah."

"Seriously?" He asks.

"I mean, it could be even sooner."

"Don't go," Sean says, "You can stay here... I mean..."

"What else am I supposed to do? This is what I know, my life."

"Fuck Jaleel, you don't know what else to do? How stupid are you?"

"Stupid enough." I say.

"No... fuck ... it's... I mean... it's just that, well, we worry, and everything seemed so normal again, like it was going well, and working, and now... now, now it's..." Sean walks away, into the living room, sets himself down on the couch, rolls his head back, and sighs.

"It's not much to debate, I don't have anything to say. It's what I'm doing." I say.

Sean turns to me, shakes his head, "It doesn't matter anyway." He stands, walks to an understated oak liquor cabinet. Kneels, considers, picks something, then stands and walks to the kitchen. He acquires 2 glasses from the cabinet, from his freezer he pulls out two specialized ice molds, breaks the ice free from each and puts them in the glasses. He pours heavy drinks. "It's a 21 year old Nikka, Tah-Ket, Ta-kit; fuck it, anyway it's something nice."

I sip the the whiskey, we sit in silence.

"You're using the spherical mold I got you." I say.

"Yeah. It's nice. Feels classy."

"I was flying back from, shit, I don't remember, but I was in Tokyo airport and I saw them… What was that, like 6 or 7 years ago?" I ask

"Yeah, we were kids." Sean says.

Sean laughs, "I was so fucking proud you got me that. This simple fucking sphered ice mold and I was ecstatic." Sean shakes his head, "I felt like you were showing faith in me, that you somehow knew one day I'd be classy enough to be expected to have such a thing." Sean says. "I still have all the postcards you sent."

We take a drink together. I shake my glass, watch the whiskey get agitated. The ball of ice bounces around against the glass, sounding like muted chimes. Some of the amber gold splashes on my thumb. I suck it off.

The whiskey is caramel, oak-like, smooth.

Easy.

Looking at Sean, his loose, long limbs, that soft smile...

And I think:

Remember him like that.

And we drink more.

"J, I love you, but I don't support this choice."

"Ok." I say.

"Good luck, anyway." He says. We drink to ourselves. The night fades out, and nothing more is really said. It's all passing, anyway.

I can sense he is hurt. It surprises me. Not sure what surprises me, but I feel the surprise.

I don't want to explain it. I don't know how to articulate the pain of investing, knowing that someone cares, has hopes designated for you; and all of it, only and always, gets washed to the sea, and back around again, how do I explain that?

That it's all hopeless, give in. Give up.

But.

I don't feel that either.

It's more subtle, a feeling I know would be foreign to Sean: you feel so numbed you have to walk that thin line to feel alive. You know life there, when the adrenaline floods you, and every moment is stretched; relative, right?

It's the closet thing I have to living.

And while here, sipping fine whiskey with an old friend, I hear you telling me: It's not a way to live.

Well, it's all I got; and I'm going to try and live it.

LIFE IS NOT A WAY-STATION

Two more days and I leave. Sean and I hardly speak. It feels heavy. Anyway — I guess it's easier, quietly everything happens, then it's done. It feels less like a wreckage that way.

While Sean works, I carefully tie-up all loose ends (all but Zoë, she remains loose), sit alone, read. Hemingway resonates with me right now. His lonely, concise prose feels nice.

At night: I wander Seattle. Some nights, like tonight, I drink. Tonight: Liberty Bar in the North Hill. The place is small, long like a rail car. Large mirrored walls double the interior's appearance.

Terrance, the barkeep, recognizes me. He walks over, big smile leading. He's got brilliant white teeth and a boyish face.

"J, what a surprise."

"Yeah, I'm taking in the sights before flying out again."

Terrance grins, "Where to now?"

"Israel." I say.

"What's that like?"

"Intense."

"I guess … I mean," He pauses, tries to fathom, gives up, "You'd have to be right? To live there? With everything going on…" He looks to me, "Right?"

I don't answer, his thought lingers … I think: You have to want to live, because everything is dying, and over there you see it close: go to school and work and home with it, and once you want to live it's intense. Eventually I indulge him with a nod.

"Can I get a nice Japanese whiskey?" I ask.

Terrance looks relieved with to have the subject changed, he let's out a quiet almost imperceptible sigh, "Got a little secret, I'll share it with cause you're leaving… it's a special Nikka … a friend brought it from Tokyo. Can't find it here." He smiles, "Hold on."

He shuffles off, smiling and chatting with other patrons. His stocky body filling empty space at each table he stops at. He seems content. Maybe that's the key? Find space to be comfortable. I'm comfortable being uncomfortable.

Terrance returns with a simple bottle.

"It's woody, has a clean wood taste, almost like a nice bourbon but not as thick." Two glasses appear, he tips the bottle and the amor liquid slides into each. Together we sniff, smile, clink, thanks, and drink.

The first sip is nice, succulent almost. Feel nourishing. I know it's not, but it feels. Maybe that's the problem? I find nourishment in the vice.

To Nick, I nod, "A full glass please." I ask.

Terrance laughs, pleased, pours into my glass with a glad and heavy hand, "Not for you tonight!" He says, pats my shoulder.

Treatment like a hero. I'm nobodies hero. Terrance returns to the bar, leaves me alone. Alone, again, like always. Every sip a reminder. How'd I end up here? You'd tell me it's my own damn fault and I'd smile sheepishly and I'd know you were right.

But right or wrong doesn't provide solace the same way barrel aged ethanol does. What takes 15 years gone in ten minutes. As appreciation I order another. There was a scene like this in The Little Prince, right Zoë? Yes, there was, but she's not telling me about it. I'll tell myself about it. It was a lonely drunk, drunk because he's lonely and lonely because he's drunk. I'm not lonely, I'm insulated. Just in case, I send out a text. In five minutes a text returns: I'll see you there shortly.

LET IT HIT YOU ON THE WAY OUT.

She arrives and my heart constricts.

I almost panic.

I closed the door gently on Zoë. Did she know that?

Laurie arrives. I see her. She hasn't found me just yet.

I could walk away, still. I know that this ... this ... would slam the door.

I signal to Laurie. I'm going to slam the door.

Why?

You know damn well why.

You don't?

I know.

Do I?

I must know. Otherwise, what the fuck am I doing?

IT'S NOT THE FOOLS WHO ARE IN LOVE.

No space for doubt. Forward. Never Backward. Past is an illusion. No it's not, you yell at me. It has to be.

Laurie glides right next to me, kisses my cheek.

"What are you drinking?" She asks.

"A Nikka. It's almost a Japanese Bourbon." I say.

"Impossible." She says.

"Very much so possible," I say, handing her the glass.

Her slender fingers hold the glass up, examine the liquid, carefully, like a get trader might, "Nice color," she says, closing her eyes, bringing the glass lip to her nose and inhaling. The glass distorts her lipstick mouth, and I think Zoë never wore make-up. I liked that, the present beauty, Laurie does wear make-up. It's fitting; mask of the night washes away in the morning. She sips, and the bourbon glistens, clinging to her deep red lips.

"It's nice," She says.

"It is."

"Order me one?"

Terrance returns when he sees my companion. He puts his hand on my shoulder, smiles broadly, I have his approval. Of course I do. Laurie is beautiful. A full formed temptress. Devil in a dress or some such shit. Are you the Devil, Laurie? I'd give you my soul for solace. But the devil gives no solace. Neither does God. God has only suffering for you. It's just like in Jobs Story, God showing the devil he's right. Gambling god, god gambling on making humans, and giving us claws. Not claws, but minds to build weapons. Weapons like: deep red lipstick. Fuck it, Laurie is probably just as human as me, and neither of us want to know what that means. Two more drinks are ordered.

Terrance brings them with a wink. Laurie grips my bicep with her claws, "Drink up," She says.

"Cheers," Look her in the eyes when you cheer, take a sip, straight no chaser; always. Always know your poison.

"So you missed me." Laurie says.

"Something like that I guess." I say.

"Still have a partner?" She asks.

"Would it matter?" I ask.

"It might."

"Ok." I say, "Well, I don't think I do."

"What's that mean?" She asks.

"I left."

"Left?" She waits, "I don't understand."

"I left." I don't clarify.

Laurie looks at me, the whiskey in her hands, thinks, "Ok," She accepts.

Together we drink quietly, watching the bar patrons. A few couples, domestic spectrum of bliss and neglect... a birthday, how many before you stop drinking at bars with friends? ... A muted crowd mostly.

"Why'd you contact me, really?" She asks.

"I fly out to Israel tomorrow."

"Trip?"

"No. Work."

"Fashion Stuff."

I don't answer, shake my head.

She considers it. "You plan on coming back to Seattle?"

"No plans. Not Really."

Laurie drinks. "That's ok." She says.

"Ok?"

"Yeah, I don't mind."

"That's good."

Laurie smiles, "Cut and dry, right?"

"Cut and dry." I say.

Feeling the whiskey. Pay Terrance for the last two. Step outside with Laurie, stars out and glorious; I'm not as glorious as the light of the distant past exploding through the sky. Let's walk, excellent idea. Through Volunteer park, chit chat. Little Histories. She tells me how the city tried to put cameras here to catch the naughty gays playing doctor in the bushes. I tell her concerns and fears. I can give her them, like an empty reservoir. I hear hers. I can be her reservoir.

"I feel drunk," I say. I inhale the smell of firs, pines, fresh grass, cold wind.

"Cocaine?" She asks.

"Sure."

She looks around, digs through her bag, opens a small plastic bag, scoops white powder out with a little spoon on her keychain. I lean in, snort.

"I bet it was an odd meeting at city hall, the first time they proposed putting cameras in the park ..." I say.

"Imagine an old ass man frothing at the mouth, yelling about those sexual deviants and criminals." Laurie laughs, grins. That sweet grin.

She grips my bicep, "What the hell makes you so indifferent?" She asks.

"Time, I guess."

"Bullshit, time is indifferent, it doesn't make you indifferent though, it doesn't make you anything but older because it doesn't give a shit." She snarks.

Thinking about her question, there are answers, and I'd much rather ignore them.

"It is what it is." I say.

"That's just a cheap tautology."

"I don't really have more depth for you... but that's why you're here right? Cause if I ask you same question you don't have an answer, or if you do, you're not telling me. It's why we're here."

Laurie tightens her face, the air becomes sharp and chillier. Then, she explodes into laughter. "Yeah, I suppose it is why were are here. But I own it. I know what a mess this, and I won't be the naive fool that invest in a man like you."

Zoë comes to mind. Anger, too. She's no fool.

"You're the god-damned fool." I say.

"About as much as you."

She's right.

The smart thing would be to go now, leave with a semblance of dignity. Instead we go to hers. Instead we fuck — tense, angry sex trying to waste everything inside of us. Instead we cum — temporary relief.

And like that I leave. First her home, but really, Seattle. I leave. All I feel is numbness.

THE MAN IN THE MOON IS NOT ONE FOR LAUGHTER.

No one takes me to the airport. Go into the world, alone, come out ... or some such cliché.

In the airport, through ticket lines and security, the whole idle chaos and pageantry, and I'm starting to feel less murky. It's the facsimile of purpose — high-wire distraction.

At the terminal, rain on the windows, watching the buzzing on the tarmac. Routine work for movement and escape, and the rain feeling like it is washing everything away.

Zoë is in my mind. Her messages haunting. If you're haunting me, I must be haunting you. I tried to write it to her. I tried to say it. I send her a letter. I didn't ask for forgiveness... but I crave understanding.

Turning now to the travelers. They busy themselves, anxious energy, trying to be comfortable in-between. Not many people are comfortable in the spaces between, it's too ambiguous. Some are.

A little girl, maybe 4 or 5 smiles at me. She's got curly hair, mocha skin. She smiles at me as if I meant something. I wonder if its true, that there is magic in children. Is there magic in you? Something more than dreary intercoms, sheepish passengers and lives lived half dead. Better to be all dead, right? Or is a half-life enough?

My new friend doesn't have the answer. She shakes her curls, laughs, hides her face behind hands, runs in a circle, screams, then laughs again.

"You have laughter like the sun." I say to her.

She looks at me.

"Not like the moon's, the moon laughs like the tide, lifting you, dropping you, then leaving you empty."

She turns away from me.

To laugh like the sun is to have warmth, and growth.

To laugh like the moon is to purge, and erase.

My new friend, she'll laugh both ways. I hope you never lose one or the other, I think.

CAN YOU EVER GET FAR ENOUGH?

Passengers begin to board as the the first privileged few are called forward. I wait till the end. Walking slowly, every step regret-heavy.

The footfall sounds like the drum of a funeral march.

A soft empty beat.

A heart beat.

Empty hearted and cold.

I want to sing a song, a lonely melody. Bob Dylan said it once, say it again: I was alright, till I fell in love with you.

There are no love songs at a funeral.

Inside the metal belly.

Take my seat, in a daze.

Settle, in a daze.

A hazy daze, hazy days ahead. Door shuts, buckle up, we're moving. Get ready to take-off. I'm not ever coming back, and I laugh, like the moon. The tide pulls you down. Laugh now, to erase everything, to survive.

PUFFER FISH ARE POISONIOUS.

Final destination: Ben Gurion Tel Aviv International Airport.

The screens telling us where the luggage will end up says its 39 degrees Celsius outside. Between the sweltering outside and me is a stern faced Arab man asking me rapid fire interrogative style questions. He fondles my passport, knowing I'm not just a tourist, "Purpose?"

"Journalism." I say.

"Explain."

"I take photos."

"Of what?"

"What I'm told." I don't tell him of what. We both know of what. He doesn't like it. Well, neither do I… and everyone has an interest in image control, but, bravery for show means nothing if nothing is gained. Deflate myself, look small and inconsequential. I require entry into this fine establishment, good sir.

A second officer arrives. Number 2 is tall, his smile is stiff, posture intractable. He looks Russian.

"You have all your papers, yes?" Number 2 asks.

"Actually he does," I motion to the stout Arab that is Number 1.

Number 1 hands them over to number, glaring at me the whole time. Number 2 grabs the papers, his gaze lingering on me, studying me. He holds my paperwork for a few minutes before looking it over.

Number 2's head down, idle chatter, not idle, "What do you think of all the … terrorism? Terrible, no? You have seen it, I am sure, how cruel they are."

"I don't think much. I'm not paid for that." I say.

"You're funny, huh? Ok, ok, ok… you've been here before, yes?"

"Yes, same then as well."

Number 2 nods, "You have friends here?"

"A few. One good one. His name is Tal, lives in Tel Aviv. He was a sniper for you guys."

Number 2 relaxes, just a little, "Will you visit this friend?"

"That's my general plan. I'm staying with him for the week before I start work."

"He is Israeli?"

"Yes."

Number 2's smile loosens. He hands me various visas and paperwork, fondles my passport, hands it over to me, "Yes, Ok."

Number 1 watches it all, smug and satisfied, "Your friend will show you a good time in the city before work." He says.

"Thanks." I say, as I walk through, officially inside the borders of the Holy Milk and Honey Land.

GOING BACK IS WHAT KILLED THE NOTORIOUS B.I.G.

Tal is waiting for me at the baggage carousel. He wears aviator Ray-Bans, with the gold frames, a Lacoste polo shirt, a wild patterned sailing short. His 5 foot 5 frame is athletic as ever.

"The gold frames match your beautiful brown skin," I say, "Still, you look like an asshole wearing them indoors."

"Ya ya, we go, quickly." He grabs my belongings, barely pauses for me to grab my waiting bags, and rushes out.

The heat hits me right away, and I get lightheaded, but Tal pushes me on, stopping at a Red Fiat. It's parked illegally, "Come on, come on, Yala!" he says, throwing my things into the back seats.

Once my things are away he embraces me, "You Mother Fucker, it's long time. Come we go," He pushes me into the car, gets into the driver seat, "You need food? Beer? Hashish? Pot, maybe? I have hashish, but if you want pot I get pot.. Eh, what did you like, whiskey? You still like it? We get you whiskey."

"Shit, Tal, one step at a time."

"Ok, ok." He pulls out of the arrivals lane and speeds off.

"You come at bad time. Lots of rockets, many." Tal says.

"Hmm, Lucky me."

Tal laughs, "You're a funny mother fucker."

"Funnier with food and beer… give me those and I'll give you a dinner show."

Tal laughs harder, "Funny funny mother fucker." He smiles.

"Comedy hour." I say.

"What you want to eat?" Tal asks.

"Something boozy and something tasty." I say.

"Yah, ok. I take you somewhere nice, ok?" Tal says.

"Whatever." I say. Smile.

For a moment I feel loose, the general tension of life unraveling. Tal drives and we don't speak, leaving Ben Gurion behind, entering the arterial series of freeways, heading towards Tel Aviv. Windows open, the sun hot, always hot, and the radio plays a reggae rag-time beat with Hebrew rapping.

Tal is bouncing, "This is shit, man, it's so fucking nice," He says.

"It's alright." I say.

"You no like?"

"It's alright."

"Mother fucker, you don't like, ok, something else, I have it." Tal fiddles with his phone, plugs it into the an auxiliary cord, and picks something, "Biggie, Mother Fucker."

I laugh, "Ok."

"'Yeah, ok,' you always say this... yeah, ok ..." Tal admonishes, "You have to commit mother fucker."

"Yeah, ok." I say.

Tal laughs, "Mother Fucking Seinfeld." Biggies' voice begins the famous refrain, 'going, going back back to Cali Cali" and Tal raises the volume, rapping along in stuttering Israeli accented English.

I laugh, rifle through my back-pack, find sun-glasses, put them on. It's almost too perfect.

Tal pulls off the the highway, just at the edges of Tel Aviv, he drives towards the Mediterranean, finds parking, and stops the car. A beach-bar, called Pura Vida is in front of us. Letting out a whoop, "Here we are, best food, best drinks, my friend owns it."

"Great, I hope her has beer." I say.

Tal laughs, "Yes yes, beer, whiskey, whatever you like."

Inside is dark wood, repurposed surfboard masquerading as shelves and tables; Dub-Reggae is playing.

"Ranni!" Tal shouts.

A tall muscular man steps forward.

"Eh?" He squints, "Tal? Tal!"

A rapid fire conversation in Hebrew unfolds. Ranni and Tal all eager smiles. Tal pulls me forward, "Hey, Big J, I tell Ranni what you do, and about you, he invite us to stay and drink, ok?"

"What you drink?" Ranni asks.

"Coffee, water, beer, whiskey." I say.

Ranni laughs, turns to Tal "He is funny man." Turning back to me, "We have all of this, what kind you want now?"

"The good kind." I say.

Ranni laughs harder, "The good kind... I love this, yes. The good kind! Always the good kind."

Still chuckling, Ranni turns and yells something to a vacant eyed woman. She looks at us blandly, nods, and lazily gets up.

"I tell her to bring us a whiskey that grows hairs and Turkish coffee that loses hairs."

"Keep it even." I say, "I'm guessing it's your bar?"

"Yeah, yeah, I played basketball, instead of Army, and then I hurt the knee; so, I go to Costa Rica. I surf, eat mangoes, and I love it. I come home and make bar like Costa Rica. At first we slow, but now it's good. I tell you, in summer," Ranni brings all his right handed fingers to point, "it's like this ... and the girls, I tell you man, we have the prettiest girls anywhere in the world here in Israel."

"I've noticed." I say.

"How can you not." Tal says.

The waitress brings us three glasses. I sniff the glass: a strong oaky bourbon. Sip it, it's a rye.

" Dickle Rye." Ranni tells me, "I love it, because saying it is very fun."

"It's nice." I say.

"So, listen, Tal tells me you take the photos. For who?"

"Whoever pays me."

Ranni smiles, "I tell you something, here in Israel we are like Gatekeeper, ok? You understand yes? Tal tells me you have seen much... you take the photos no one takes, so you know."

"I've seen things that aren't pleasant." I say, slowly.

"Bah, unpleasant, you have seen what those brutes do, how they are..." Ranni is getting riled, "they do not act like you or me, not basic human..."

I don't respond, instead think: this is the echo repeated nightly in homes, on televisions, whispered in personal prayers.

I understand: the pain, the fear ...

Heart ache over lost friends, family here and yet to come.

An echo begging for forgiveness and hopping for justification.

Wanting justice.

Everyone wants justice for their pain.

Everyone.

Two sides and such to the coin, right?

But it's not so simple. There are more sides, and like a picture you only see what's framed; and like a picture there is a hell of a lot more happening beyond the framework.

I raise my glass to Ranni, let him have is recognition. Let them all have it, let them all be right. They can't all be right. They can all damn well be wrong. I take a quaff of bourbon, then coffee.

Tal and Ranni continue to chatter. I smile at the right moment, and they work to include me less and less. Finishing drinks, begging off a second, telling Tal and Ranni I need to unpack, rest. Tal, disappointed, tries again. I shake no.

Outside, sun burning, Tal lamely says, "He's good guy."

Inside his car, driving, "What makes you say that?" I ask.

"It's, well, sometimes he is good, and sometimes no... the thing is very confusing. You know, this is war, ok. War, all the time, and war can be hard." Tal says.

I laugh.

"What? Dis is funny?"

"War can be hard," I say, "It's simple, but true."

"Yes, this we know." He laughs.

War is hard.

LIVE WITH CHIVALRY.

At Tal's, a modest place — concrete 4 story building, drab square architecture that looks like a protective box. Inside: the entire apartment floor is tiled with a large off-white porcelain. Faded red rugs cover the living room floor.

"It's two beds, but my room-mate, he is in Argentina," Tal says. "You can take his room, it is the one on the right." Tal points to the first door down a short hallway.

Gathering my things, opening the door, the room is quaint. Posters of Reggae bands watch over the sparse white room. Only a double bed and an old drafting desk furnish it.

Tal enters the room, holding sheets and towels, "They are fresh washed, clean for you; you take a rest, and we drink tonight; little party, yes ok?"

"Ok."

He drops the sheets and towels on the bed, "Wait, ok?" He steps out.

I don't bother to start unpacking. I lazily start to make the bed. Tal returns with a blue-glass pipe in his hands, "Hashish?" he offers.

Assenting, taking the pipe, lighting it, inhaling the smoke, letting it out, "Nice to see you again, friend." Tal says.

"Yes, nice," I say.

He leaves me in peace, pipe still in my hands. I take one more hit, then set the pipe down on the drafting table. The faces of Reggae band members smile on. I lay down after undressing, it's warm.

Mind is racing. Quiet down. It won't. I'm not thinking about what's to come, the multiple dangers and challenges, I'm thinking about Zoë.

I already know about what's to come. But Zoë … I don't fully know what's gone.

The next few hours pass and no rest comes. Tal knocks, "J, Party time, ok, yes?"

Groaning, "Sure." I say.

He opens the door, beer in hand, offering it.

Taking it. Swallowing some. Feels nice.

"Ok, Tal, take me to party." I say.

"Yes, yes, ok, ok." Tal pats my back.

In his kitchen, sparse, clean. A bottle of Chivas sits front and center.

"You like this, no?" He asks.

"I did." I say.

"No more?" He asks.

"Sure," I shrug, "More." I smile, too, touched that he remembers. Strange the impressions we leave in our wake, I think, watching the Chivas pour into a tumbler.

Gracefully accepting the drink, taking a sip; feeling it spread warmth. Feeling it take me back to my third field assignment, in Turkey. Protests were raging — the push of religion, the pull of democracy, contrasting ideas, tension between competing visions.

Peter, I was working with Peter Travers, a journalist and caustic curmudgeon. Loved Chivas. Every night he insisted we share it. I did happily. Me, young, starting, and he the gnarled veteran. Four years later I heard he committed suicide. His fourth or fifth wife had left him. Peter, always the romantic, craving connections, never knowing how to create the foundations to keep them.

I'm averse. Suspicious.

Or maybe not.

You'd call me a fool.

Insist that the failures of others are not my own to carry.

Maybe. Maybe you're right.

But I'd just as soon not carry anything.

To break the lull, I tell Tal, "I used to have a friend who loved this."

"Yea…" Tal says.

I think, how to fill this in. Let it die, instead. Like Peter.

"Thank you, Tal." I say.

He smiles, megawatt smile, brilliant and inviting, "Yes," He says, hugging me, gripping me, "I have friend who likes Chivas." Tal laughs.

Feeling good now, at least, distant from Zoë; not plagued. It's the little pleasures, that's all I get, that is all I'm allowed.

"Let's go." I say

"Party!" Tal shouts.

HERE'S LOOKING SOMEWHERE, KID.

Arriving at a rectangular concrete building. It's parking structure chic. A few people are loitering outside, some young skateboard kids with slightly humped shoulders, two girls with colored hair and a flask between them; everyone is smoking. One of the girls says something to Tal in a soft casual way. He laughs, but continues walking on.

At the door we meet a slim and tall man, disheveled as a matter of style. Tal introduces him as Benyamin. Benyamin in turn introduces us to the door girl, Mimi, who asks for our id. Tal says something to Benyamin who waves us in, nodding at Mimi, who shrugs and lets us through.

Inside is lit by l.e.d. tubes wrapped around a few iron sculptures and Chinese laters that hang from steel rafters. There is a makeshift bar, a DJ booth on a simple table, and a jovial free-for-all feel to the space. It's around one a.m. now, so things are just picking up in pace.

The bar is pushy, getting a drink is a process only a New Yorker might love. The tender smiles at me, follows my english, then pours me the right whiskey. Tal pays over my objections and we turn to the open space, fortified.

Tal scans the room, finds his friends, and leads me for introductions to a smiling group of young hipsters. All of them are welcoming. Tal starts introductions — Galli is a stout goateed man who bounces with each step and word he expels, and Dar a tall Russian with the deliberateness of a mountain, and ... — but Tal quickly distracted and leaves me to fend for self.

A green eyed woman introduces herself to me first, "You are Tal's friend, from America."

"Yes." I say.

"I am Tal's friend too. He is like brother, this you understand, yes?"

"I do now…" I say, "Well, we have something in common then."

She laughs. Something about dry wit appeals to the Israelis… maybe it's directness, maybe concepts like rudeness fall away when dying is very real possibility.

I ask her where she is from. Moroccan and French she tells me. I accept that as an answer. Her name is Chen, said in that unique guttural poetic way of Arabic. She takes my short honest answers as budding intimacy. It's easy to let her since I don't care.

Her mother is Jewish, from Paris. Her father is muslim, born in Marrakesh, raised from 16 in Paris. She tells me their story — a variation of rich-girl, poor-boy, wrong side of the tracks, right side of love, and rebellion makes babies.

Families fight, debating the fate of the fetus. Disgrace on all sides, everyone pointing fingers except for the grandmother on her mother's side, the one in Israel; so that's where they go.

Nine months later and disputes dissipate, giving way to a wailing baby girl named Chen and real concerns.

"So we lived with my Great-Bubbe, in Ashkelon on a farm, in a house we all build together."

I imagine Chen as a child, scampering with tools in hand, her great-grandmother directing the build, the hard scrapple pioneer seeking refuge from a world that had turned away from her people — because any nations excuse is a paltry comfort against systemic cruelty.

I ask Chen about the army, if being Muslim and Jewish mattered much. She doesn't understand my question.

"… Maybe they treated you differently? Or …." I ask again.

"No, I am like the same."

"What about being in the army, I mean… does it change your reasons for fighting."

"This is my home, I fight for home." She says, her face momentarily sour.

I wonder about Palestinians. If they feel the same. Of course they do.

"It's not religion." She says.

It probably isn't. But religion claims this home for both of them.

I stop asking, instead say I want air. Chen smiles, invites me to the roof.

"Come, all the air you need." She says.

"Ok, let me get a drink first."

Get a beer, follow her up 3 flights of stairs, then a fire ladder with one missing rung, finally emerging in the crisp night. Others are already here, laughing gently, no moon tonight and a sliver of the Mediterranean is visible in the background.

Historical folk-lore says Phoenician traders discovered glass on the beach over there, while trying to cook dinner on saltpeter stone. That was some 5,000 years ago.

Like this conflict.

History looming & living — taken for granted.

It's easy to take history for granted, life is short, and the music continues below, and before you know it beer is gone too.

People around us seem to be happy, appreciate each moment. Chen reaches for my hand, she's trying to find something to hold onto.

I'm looking at her trying to find Zoë—history looming and living.

I let go of Chen.

She wants comfort I can't offer.

Chen steps closer, hugs me. I feel cold against her, staying for a moment, just a moment, till the fire door opens and the sound of jovial laughter precedes familiar faces; Tal and friends see us, yes, we are doing wonderful, mellow man, the night is lovely, sure I'll have another… and in a long blur carousing till dawn.

Chen seeks me one last time, and I can't, I can't, I turn away. I'm not even capable of temporary remedies.

She's not what I want.

What do you want?

Zoë.

I had her.

I left her.

Did I lose her?

I'm lost.

Dawn rises, and Tal and I leave, stopping for greasy breakfast before returning to Tal's home.

ME AND JULIO, DOWN BY THE SCHOOLYARD

Drinking black mint tea on the small balcony of Tal's apartment. He's talking fast, excited. The sun isn't even in mid-sky yet the heat is brutal. It's supposed to be spring.

The heat's refraction distorts a school, a playground, and a grocers — the various signs of life built carefully — community, imperfect and normal.

"How does everyone do it?" I ask

"Do what?" Tal asks.

"Live."

"Is this joke?" Tal asks.

"No, I mean living in war."

"You know, you have done this too. You get used to it."

"Sure." I sip tea, considering the tranquil scene.

"Chen likes you." Tall says.

"Sure," I say.

"Sure, sure, he says," Tal shakes his head, "She is beautiful Israeli girl, I tell you good persons too. Sure, sure, sure… this fuckin' idiot."

"I'm an idiot, but it's not that simple." I say.

"Oh, you have woman?"

"Maybe? No, not anymore."

"Why not?"

"I told you you were right, I'm an idiot." I say.

Tal laughs. "Yes, you are. A sure idiot."

A bell rings, the school has a recess. Children flood out of the concrete building to the playground. They dash from one end to the other, lazily watched by a women in conservative clothing.

"I don't miss all that. School, teachers."

Tal looks at the playground "She is Orthodox, not so much… but yes, Orthodox" he says, "But she wears more modern clothing, just a little, because some parents do not like this… too religious."

"I don't miss the times either, ever day scary, big world… now, now is more fun. I understand more of life."

I agree.

"How long you staying?" He asks.

"Two more days. I go to Jerusalem"

"Two days?"

"Two days."

We continue to watch the children in silence until they are rounded up and ushered inside.

"And then to Gaza?" Tal asks.

"To Gaza." I say.

Tal reaches sideward, grips my shoulder, "When you are back, break or done, you come stay again."

"Sounds nice." I say.

ALL YOUR THEORIES ARE
PROBABLY WRONG, TOO.

Arriving in Jerusalem, stifling hot day, spice scented air as I get off the bus. Soldiers casually litter the street, familiar, part of the landscape with orthodox jews, and the common citizen. Vendors shout from small alleyways, hocking from carts and storefronts against the aged limestone.

Hail a cab, get in, give him an address. The driver is rotund and bald, with exaggerated mannerisms and an aggressive english.

Looking at me from his mirror, he studies.

"American," He asks.

"Uh huh." I say.

He snorts, a harsh phlegmatic sound.

"And, uh, what you do?" He asks.

"Take pictures."

He snorts, again, I see him squinting into the rearview mirror.

"Of what?" He asks.

"Models." I say.

The man grins, "Like pretty girls in the bathing suits?"

I give him a languid nod yes.

He claps his hands, "Good, good. We have pretty girls here, prettiest in world." He says.

"At first I think you are journalist. I don't like them, All of them, they tell stories and make us like terrorist, but not all of us is terrorist."

"That's unfortunate." I say.

"I'm from Jordan." He points proudly at himself, "Muslim!" He looks at me for a reaction. I have none. "I am like you, I drive cab, I have family."

I nod. The taxi stops at a red light. He turns to face me with an awkward half body twist. "I tell you, the real trouble, it is the Jews... the Orthodox. They only want the land, they only take the land. They want us out, all of us." His voices raises, face an ugly contortion, "They want power and money and land."

I say nothing.

He calms.

"Not all Jews are so bad, you understand? Only the religious ones, they are different ... like pigs. Eating power. Power hungry pigs."

I still say nothing.

There is no use in trying to discuss the finer points of conflict. People want simple stories with easy villains. Mr. Cabbie has his: the black coat jews and their secret study sessions on strategy to control it all.

It's an old narrative, and for him it fits. The same re-cast story of the world-owning zionist — start with banks and media and...

Fuck.

What tiresome tripe people believe.

Tiresome tripe people insist on sharing.

Tiresome tripe people die for.

Stupid.

Cabbie expounds further. Complex theories, ideas grandiose and continually stupid.

Thankfully, we reach Rae's apartment. Paying the man, emptying my own bags from the trunk, watching him drive off, content to be alone.

I open my phone, follow messaged instructions to a mounted steel box beside a simple iron door. Press the combination I was told. A sleepy voice answers, recognizes my own, and then a loud buzzing noise follows. I enter into a small foyer, surrounded by limestone. A set of stairs to my left.
Rae is descending the stairs. Elegant in a loose top and sweats, she smiles sheepishly down at me. Her wispy, dissolved nonchalance is beautiful.

"Welcome." She says, words drawn from sleep.

"I thought I emailed you my arrival time?" I ask.

"You did." She nods, leading me up the stairs.

"Least it's not my fault then."

"No, it's not your fault. It is Yael's fault, or, I guess my own. Though, I suppose, I could blame the wine bottle Yael brought over ... she likes wine." She says.

"So do you." I say.

Rae nods, at the end of three flights, she comes to a large wooden door. With her key she opens it.

We enter a large, airy space. Almost a dance studio. The interior wall where windows are is of ancient limestone. There is a kitchen in the corner of the open room, almost an annoyed afterthought. Large windows let light flood in. One is stained glass. I put my stuff down.

"This place was last publishing house for talmudic texts." Rae tells me. "Commentary and the text itself."

She goes to the kitchen and pours herself a glass of water. Asks if I want a cup. I take one. "I like it, living here... for some reason living where they printed all that religious shit makes me feel safe."

I laugh, "What does Yael think?"

"It creeps her out a little when we fuck, but it sort of turns her on at the same time. Like the sacred and profane... otherwise she doesn't care."

Rae glides across the room and seats herself on a white-leather L-shaped couch.

I follow her lead.

"Are you still seeing that english dude... Robert?"

"Roger." She clarifies.

"Yeah."

"No, for our 2 year anniversary I told Yael I'd honestly try monogamy."

I snort.

Rae smiles at me, "Neither of us think it will last, but we think of it as this temporary exercise in foundation building. Build trust and what not."

"And what not."

"It's good for now." She shrugs.

"Good for now is good enough." I say.

Rae stretches herself out, her long thin frame draping over the couch, "And so, internal question and all: is now good for you?"

"Mmmm." I shrug.

"So no," She says, "That means no."

"Astute."

She shrugs, "I know you. We've been friends long enough."

"Sure."

"Want to expand?"

"No."

"Later?"

"Maybe."

"Something else, then?"

"Something else." I say.

Rae yawns, expanding herself in the process, then turning to face me from her back to sitting, seamless and graceful, "Hangovers. Fuck hangovers. It's brutal and I'm getting old."

"Can I ask you something?"

Rae nods.

"How did you adjust? I mean... writing about the camps, some of those stories... and rape ... and; it's brutal, and now you're painting, being normal. How did you do that?"

Rae gets up, walks to the kitchen, pours herself fizzy water, adds vodka and a squeeze of lime, "Anything to kill this hangover," She says.

Drink in hand, sitting back down, now across from me on the diagonal.

"I didn't." She says, "Not really. I mean we I've in a city on knifes edge always, I can't commit to anything but work,

I'm close to 35 and afraid of owning things and it's not some enlightened posturing about possessions either."

"But you haven't gone back. You've been with Yael for 5 or 6 years now."

"True."

"It's like an addiction." I say, "And it fucks you up."

Rae studies me, "I guess I got tired of it. I just couldn't keep going."

"How'd you know you were done?"

"I was writing a story about this girl who had been beaten and raped from trying to go to school, it was devastating and I couldn't finish it. I spent 3 days drinking, and on coke and ketamine, and then I just stopped. I just stopped. I was in this haze for 6 months or so."

"Then what?" I ask.

"Then? Then I woke up, and decided I was done."

She pauses, drinks, closes her eyes, takes a deep breath in. Her out breath is heavy.

"That's it? You woke up?"

She nods, "Painting helped. Self expression is therapy or some such."

"That's it?"

"You don't get it still. It never leaves you. Never. It's there always. Always. Till death do you part...but, you don't have to live in it. Do that and you'll wither. Fuck, J, it's why we forget. You just have to forget somethings to live."

We both take a drink, sit back.

Rae stands, "I love you, J, and I'm tired now. I'm hungover and tired and I'm going to take a nap. Yael will be in for dinner, she wants to see you. Make yourself at home."

Rae walks down a hallway to her bedroom, opens the door and stops, "All men are so fucking romantic," she says, "you make these romantic caricatures of life and war and pain and then force yourself to live it."

"Why can't it be some romantic comedy instead of a romantic tragedy then? Like I can be Hugh Grant." I say, chuckling.

"I don't know, J. Ask yourself." She closes her door, leaving me alone.

I hear the latch, I slump on her couch, I start to cry.

LOT'S WIFE CRIED HERSELF INTO A PILLAR OF SALT.

Waking up on Rae's couch, the light of the day is just a hard grey now. Rae's tender silhouette is shuffling around the kitchen.

"Yael will be here any moment." She tells me, "Care for a drink?"

"Sure."

"Tea?" She asks.

"Beer?"

"Tea." Rae gently insists.

"Fine, what kind?"

"Black tea with fresh mint," She says, handing me the mug.

"What's for dinner?"

"Yale is making falafel for us, it's a treat."

"Lovely." I say, sipping my tea.

The door opens and a slim, fierce woman enters. Her curls are equally fierce, ending at her shoulders.

"Yael." I say, standing to greet her.

"Jaleel," She meets me with a resounding hug, pulling away, hand clasped to my shoulder, "You are good, yes?"

"Enough." I answer.

"Bah, enough, you look alive yes? That is more than enough."

"Yael," Rae grabs Yael's shoulder.

"Nikud," Yael says. They embrace, kiss.

Yale turns back to me, "I go cook, ok, but do talk. Tell me all about this enough." She kisses my cheeks and heads to the kitchen.

Rae grins at me, silly and open and content.

"The tea is nice," I offer.

Rae chuckles, "Hmm, I know."

It's silent, just a tic, as Rae basks in her love for Yael and I consider what that love is.

"It's nice," I say, "what you have."

She smiles, like a dope.

"What do you think of dreams," I ask, uncomfortable.

Rae blinks, "Think of them? I don't."

"I mean, do you think they are important? Some subconscious cry for help?" I ask.

"I don't know, I don't dream that much. I guess, if I had to say anything, they're just expressions of anxiety, things we can't or don't face head on."

"Logical," I grunt.

"Why do you ask?"

I shrug, "No reason."

Rae looks at me, "I don't believe you, but I'll leave it alone."
I think about what she said: what am I am not facing.

What's chasing me?

Yael calls from the kitchen. We go. A wonderful spread is laid out, bight vibrant colors of Israeli cuisine painting the table.

"Sit, sit, sit, eat, eat, eat." Yael practically sings, "I go get wine."

"No, you sit, I go." Rae is already on her way.

Yael sits across from me. "She is like to pretend that she is fancy, her and her wine." Yael says, chuckling.

I smile sheepishly.

"But enough, tell me about this enough about enough. Tell me all things." Yael says.

"Not much to tell. I'm here for work." I say.

"No, you are have things to tell. I feel this."

"Yael, I appreciate the concern, but I can't tell you about things I don't understand." I say.

"Hmph, this is stupid. We tell the things to understand. We tell to make understanding in ourselves." Yael says, her brow furrowed, looks like a topography map, serious.

"Maybe I don't want to fuckin' talk about it." I say.

"This is stupid. You are with friends. And Rae loves you, I love you, and you are not so stupid to not know this." Yael says.

"It's none of your damn business."

"You are in my home, my guest, and so it is." Yael says, immovable.

Rae returns with a bottle, looks at each of us, "Play nice," She gently implores, placing a hand upon Yael's shoulder.

"Yes, ok." Yael nods.

"And J," She turns to me, scathing, "You arrive on our doorstep on your own morose weather pattern, and we are concerned."

She's right.

"I appreciate the concern." I say.

Rae smiles. It's almost patronizing.

"It's not easy…" I say.

…

"I just can't admit it. Saying it out loud, I mean…" I stutter, "I think I just left the first woman I've loved in a long time."

I breathe out.

Hearing it out loud — for the first time from myself — I sob, crumble into my seat. Warm salty tears pooling in my mouth. My friends comfort me. Gathering myself, drinking a cup of offered water.

Did I really run? Why?

Why?

Why the fuck did I run?

I ran. It's done.

I can't go back.

Can I?

I can't go back.

AVOID STATEMENTS WITH ALWAYS AND NEVER.

The morning crack through the curtains, slowly waking me. As consciousness washes over me, last nights break down returns. My stomach gives a jolt.

So it's this again: the pain of leaving.

First you. Then Zoë.

Everything leaves us.

I left, you'd tell me. It's the same. No, it's not, you'd say.

But the outcome is.

Groaning, lifting myself from the bed. Realizing I had the same dream again.

Get on with this life.

I can't. I will.

LOOK BOTH WAYS BEFORE CROSSING.

Phone rings 4 times before Tina answers.

"Make it ok, I see." She says.

"Well enough."

"Great, you'll meet with Paul in 2 days. He arrives tomorrow in Tel Aviv, he'll stay a night there, then you can find him at the King David Hotel. Paul's pretty organized and will have most of the details you need. Told him you were a professional."

"Aren't we all?" I ask.

"We pretend." She says.

"Thanks." I say.

Then silence.

Tina speaks first, "Jaleel…"

"Yea?"

"Careful, ok?"

"Ok."

HOLDEN CAULFIELD COULDN'T CATCH THEM ALL

In the afternoon I go for a walk in the historical district. I linger at shops, run my fingers over trinkets. Holy trinkets, useless trinkets. Stop at a small cafe where only a thin, tall morose man owner sits. He ignores me, smoking cigarettes until I order a Turkish coffee. He makes it, brings it to the table, then sits with me, offering a cigarette.

I turn him down, he lights one and begins to smoke.

"Where you from?" He asks.

"States." I say.

"Yes, ok, but from where; what part?"

"I grew up in Seattle, Washington." I sip the sludge like coffee.

"I lived in California," He says, "In West Covina."

I don't know the place.

"It's near Los Angeles." He says. He shakes his head. "I had a home, a shop, I sold walk-mans and electronics."

"This is a little different," I say.

He chuckles, then spits, "Yeah, I fucking came back. My wife was a whore and the lawyers wanted all my money, so I came back to Jordan, where I was born. Then, somehow, I'm here."

I didn't need to hear more, "Huh," Is all I offer.

He ignores my disinterest, "Jordan is a fucking funny place. Not haha, no. But I was ok, I figured it out, worked for my cousin. Then came here, wanted my own place."

We sit silently.

"I got arrested, you know." He says.

"For not paying your lawyers?" I say.

He waves a hand at me, laughs, "No, no, no, no." He pauses — I hope we are done — "The Israelis man, they fucking arrested me."

"Sucks." I say.

"They fucking beat me man, kept me living in my own shit. Over nothing. Little things, but because I was Jordanian ... the pricks would laugh at me. Throw their lit cigarettes at me..." He's getting angry.

I let his tirade continue.

"You know what that is like? Fucking torture, I mean real torture..." He shakes his head. Looks ready to cry, looks ready to yell, looks anguished. A shaky hand lights another cigarette, he inhales deeply.

"Fuck, man." Is all I say.

"Yeah, fuck man," he says, hacking and laughing at the same moment. I finish my coffee. I look into my cup, weighing another.

"I have more." He says, getting up.

"No, it's ok." I say.

He smiles, sits again, "You're a good guy," he says, "That's what the Americans say, right? Good guy..."

"What do I owe you?" I say.

He shrugs, "Nothing."

"Thanks," I say.

I get up and walk away. I walk awhile, thinking. About dreams, and home, and the shop owner, and how ugly people can be, about how vicious and wonderful it can be. I can have it all. I could have had it all. I could be so wonderful. I won't dwell, I tell myself.

Good. Bad.

It's all a spectrum.

Keep musing to myself as I watch a little girl in a yellow dress. She reminds me of you, precocious, cute. You were like that.

I'm in a dreamy lull.

Then.

Suddenly.

The noise comes first, the boom, then the hit like a huge bass blast. Disorientation. Senses scattered. Dust and heat, and I'm scrambling, looking for the little girl, inhaling smoke and the smell of nitroglycerin. Coughing. Trying to see, eyes barely opening.

Where is she? Bits of gravel kick up, burning flecks on my face. My eyes wildly flinging open, closing shut, tears at their corners. I wretch. Lungs fill with smoke as I gasp for breath. Where the fuck did she go? I hear her crying. I see her running. I don't. That's not her, it's a man with blood on him. His own, someone else's...

Is she hurt? Is she safe?

Is she safe? Is she safe? Answer me, god-damn-it.

No confirmation yet.

The dust everywhere starts to settle, the chaos of people shouting, seeking their loved ones, madness. Fear and adrenaline... and the little girl...

What am I doing?

Frantically searching for her.

Ears still ringing from the blast, I am swimming in a sea of dust, breast stroke to move forward and see, and heat, the stench of sweat and spices and blood and vomit and shit, and frantic bodies, moaning, crying, running, seeking.

Am I ok?

I'm ok.

It's quieter now.

What am I doing here?

Searching amidst the bodies, numerous wounded people. A woman whose leg appears broken ... maybe from the blast, maybe from the stampede. She's crying, rocking back and forth, praying, crying, praying, crying. Groceries strewn on the floor, tangerines rolling as if running away. There's a teenage boy holding his arm. It looks cut open. His face is blank. Ignoring them all.

She's there. I see her. Yellow dress, sunshine, you are my sunshine.

She's laying on the ground. Curled up, scared. I run to her, stumble, trip, get up, run. My lungs burning. Heaving. I grab her, pull her into my arms. "It's ok, It's ok, It's ok, It's ok." I mutter.

Sunshine, you are my sunshine.

She's light. Easy to hold. I hug her; she's so quiet, so gentle in my arms. I exam her. The left side of her face is bloodied. She's so easy, so tender.

Sunshine, you are my sunshine.

She's not breathing. Lay her down, one, two, three, four; breathe. One, two, three, four; breathe. She's not breathing. Breathe. Just cough, sputter it up. Her mouth is bloody. Her blood is on my lips, I can taste it. One, two ... She's not breathing.

She's dead. I'm crying. She's dead.

Please don't take my sunshine away.

I carry her out of the dust. A paramedic sees us, takes her. They check her vitals, and I watch her face. The paramedic taps me, speaking quickly. I shake my head no. No. No. No.

She's dead. The paramedic confirms this. Dead.

A young woman approaches us. She sees the girl in the paramedics arms; my broken look. Her face is wild, disbelieving. She knows. She's crying, praying, crying, praying. Like everyone. Shouting a name... I don't hear it. Then the rush as the mother comes and takes her child, and it feels as if I am thrown from the world. Dizzy and sick, I vomit. I cry and I vomit all at once. Excretions trying to rid myself of the world.

EVERYTHING EATS.

In Rae's home. Thinking about it's history: about scholars, hunched over, copying furtively, each word meant to be conveyed perfect.

Thinking about the Psalms of David, of the Song of Solomon, of Ecclesiastes.

Thinking about what walls are meant to do: save us, protect us.

Imprison us.

Walls of words, of limestone. I'm thinking about limestone, fucking limestone. I've been thinking about limestone for 2 days now, staring at Rae's living room wall, laying listless on her couch.

She forces me to eat. Drink tea. She won't let me drink hard stuff. I drink when she and Yael leave home. I drink whiskey, bourbon, whatever is at the store. My stomach is poisoned. I should stop, but I still taste the faint iron of blood. I'm trying to sanitize the taste, clean it out of my memory.

Yael implores me to sleep. She tells me, yes, yes, this life is cruel, very mean; but fuck it, fuck life, we live to say fuck it.

Rae nurses me, cold cloths on my head, gentle implorations to seek help. She tells me I moan in my sleep.

I miss my scheduled meeting with Paul. I don't care. Tina calls me constantly. Rae, one day, speaks to her in hushed tones. My phone doesn't ring again.

Without the ringing phone I'm free to keep thinking about limestone, about scholars, and ancient copyists, and hallelujah when my beloved comes, and all things under the sun.

Then it slides away into the liquor, through my belly, more poison for my liver to sort through. And momentarily I'm free, but that's a lie. I'm trying to build on that, trying to build freedom on poison in my liver and lies in my head.

Inevitably, eventually, I fall asleep. Sleep is not the pleasure dome of Xanxadoo, no morphine freedoms. I understand that, right now, just now, morphine desires.

Sleep is the same dream, on repeat. I'm at the zoo, walking through exhibits that are foggy and difficult to discern. It's grey and empty, this labyrinthian zoo. No matter what direction I take, everything leads to the South American exhibits. A small placard tells me that the center is the Jaguar exhibit. Everything leads here. Some days I go towards it, direct. Others I try and turn away and yet, whatever direction I go it leads me to the precipice of the Jaguar exhibit.

Inevitably, I look through the bars. The jaguar is savagely consuming a prey. Bloody maw, tearing into flesh. Closer examination and I recognize the prey: it's me. I'm being consumed by the Jaguar. The bright red flesh of my muscle being torn, macerated in the majestic teeth of the beautiful cat. I don't feel it, but watch fixated as my body is consumed, deliberately and with vigor by the beast. I'm being consumed. I'm being eaten alive. All I can do is watch.

LED USES LESS ELECTIRICTY THAN
THE COMMON TUNGSTEN BULB.

What am I doing here?

I know.

Sabotage.

Of myself.

YOU COULD FIGHT FOREVER OR
YOU CAN LIVE NOW.

Sabotage is easy. It allows me to believe the lies I tell myself.

I see you clearly telling me: 'You don't have to be alone, and you do everything to be alone, but you don't have to.'

Still I fight.

Why do we fight? We fight ourselves; no, we fight nature.

We fight existence because existing is too much, too Awesome.

We don't believe we deserve it.

We get angry because it's never enough.

We fight because we want more and we can't have more.

We all die. Living forever is not possible. But living now is very very possible.

WE SPEND A LIFETIME LEARNING TO HEAL

And what did I expect, coming here?

I don't know. There is the rubble, fragments of human lives; spread out like a picnic blanket.

They've stripped it all away here, the pretense, the promise, the presence.

Stripped bare, and what's left?

Take away the conflict, the demands of knowing who is right and wrong -- there is the memories, and the remainders: people trying to move on. Home is where the heart is until home is dust.

What did you leave me with? Dust. 14 years of building it up, and just like the nursery rhyme, it all falls down. And so you did. You died. My sister, dead.

Take away the pain, the conflict, the years lost to endless dark hallways of my imagination, and what remains?

I don't think it's so different, no matter who we are, what we've lost.

I've tried to tear you down and forget. What remains? Love, ever so painful, ever so present; love.

I need to heal.

Healing is forgiveness and release.

Forgive. Release.

Forgive to release: I; Forgive; You, Her, Myself ...

You: for loving me, or leaving us. You a daughter to someone.

But, more important, my sister. You my sister, I forgive.

Zoë: For penetrating to my deepest roots, shaking me, frightening me ... she needs no forgiveness, but, I hope she can forgive.

Me: I forgive myself for being afraid. Afraid of love, of letting go, of giving in. I'm going back.

I'm going back to Zoë.

I'm hoping she's still there. Hoping she still feels for me. Hoping.

Let me end with a simple truth: I love her.

Mark Mizrahi

Mark is a storyteller. Hailing from Los Angeles with an Egyptian-Jewish father and a Mexican-Catholic mother; he learned young the value of life, and has since spent life living and retelling stories of fantastical places, people, and situations.

A varied and wild life that has included studying the way fishermen interact with turtles in Ecuador and Costa Rica for the University of Washington and USAid, working as a Dominant, and learning, traveling, and progressing in street dance with world renowned poppers and tutters.

He now resides in Portland, OR., and is most proud of the beautiful friendships cultivated along the way.